COLTER'S QUEST

1622: An expedition of Spanish soldiers, carrying a hoard of gold and silver, loses its way in the mountains. Now the last man alive, Father Ignacio Corozon, hides the treasure in a cave ... 1842: Josiah Colter stumbles across that very same cave and discovers the cache ... 1888: Josiah's grandson Ben has his home burned to the ground, his wife kidnapped, and his friend killed. Chet Ballard and Jess McCall set out alongside him to find Rachel and avenge the murder ...

NEIL HUNTER

COLTER'S QUEST

Complete and Unabridged

LINFORD
Leicester

First published in Great Britain in 2016

First Linford Edition
published 2017

A catalogue record for this book is available
from the British Library.

ISBN 978–1–4448–3414–7

Published by
F. A. Thorpe (Publishing)
Anstey, Leicestershire

Set by Words & Graphics Ltd.
Anstey, Leicestershire
Printed and bound in Great Britain by
T. J. International Ltd., Padstow, Cornwall

This book is printed on acid-free paper

Prologue

Only the brittle scratching of the quill moving across the parchment broke the silence of the canyon. Tiny dust motes danced within the shimmering waves of heat, dipping and rising on gentle air currents.

High above the solid walls of ochre-colored stone hung a strip of blue-washed sky. Empty. Cloudless.

The scratching ceased. The quill paused as the writer's train of thought wandered, returning the canyon to total silence once again.

And then . . .

'God save me from this terrible place!'

1622
Father Ignacio Corozon, alone and starving, lost somewhere within the mountain fastness that would one day become

New Mexico, is writing his final thoughts in his journal. Soon after he hoped to make an attempt to walk out of the desolate mountains and seek help. He and his party had drifted north out of Mexico for more than three weeks, plagued by storms and sickness, and as the survivors hid the treasure they had taken for the glory of Spain, they all knew they would die here in this empty land.

Corozon, the last man, writes what will become his epitaph. He will never be seen alive again. He would die before he could leave the cave where he lay sick and would become, as have other members of his expedition, lost and abandoned. He will never look upon another human face, nor ever see again his beloved Spain. And the fortune in gold and silver that he and his party were transporting will become another of the legends of the Southwest.

Until one day in 1842 when a man named Josiah Colter stumbles across the cave where Corozon had concealed it before setting out on his abortive trek. The hoard had remained untouched over the decades. Lost to the world until Josiah Colter discovers it ... and unwittingly sets in motion the chain of events that will eventually involve his grandson, Ben Colter, and through their association with Colter, Chet Ballard and Jess McCall become targets ...

COLTER RANCH — NEW MEXICO TERRITORY — 1888

They saw the smoke a half mile from the spread. Easing around in his saddle Jess McCall saw the expression on his partner's face.

'Doesn't look good, son,' he said.

'Damn right it doesn't,' Chet Ballard replied and heeled his horse into motion.

With McCall close behind, Ballard pushed his horse along the downslope that brought the Colter spread into view. The house, stable and barn were burned to the ground. Charred ruins still issued some smoke. As Ballard rode across the yard he saw a sprawled figure and angled his horse towards it. He had recognized the man straight off.

It was Chey, the Chiricahua Apache who worked alongside Ben Colter. Ballard stepped from the saddle and crouched beside the still figure lying on his side. When he turned Chey over he saw the blood that marked the man's shirt. There was more blood, already drying, that had streamed down Chey's brown face from the deep wound that had split the side of his head. The Apache's eyes flickered open and he stared up at Ballard. Recognition took a few moments.

'Ballard . . . *schichobe* . . . '

'You rest easy now.'

A brown hand caught hold of Ballard's shirt.

'They took her . . . Colter's woman . . . '

'Rachel?'

Chey's head moved in a nod. 'Many of them. *Pinda Lickoyi*. They put the house to the torch. Scattered Colter's horses . . . I would have stopped them but . . . too many . . . Ballard . . . '

'Where's Colter?'

'He went to deliver horses he had broken . . . should be back later today . . . '

'Quite a bunch was here,' McCall

said from behind his partner. 'Six. Maybe more. Hard to tell. But I can see where they rode out. Direction they took.'

'They say why?' Ballard asked.

Chey didn't answer. He had lapsed into unconsciousness.

Ballard's mind was full of confused thoughts as to what needed doing. He pushed to his feet, glancing around at the devastation. Made his choice.

'Jess, go see if you can find one of the stray horses.'

McCall swung his mount around and spurred it across the yard, picking up the hoofprints left by the horses that had been driven from the open corral.

Taking his canteen from the saddle and a cloth from his saddlebags Ballard returned to where Chey lay and cleaned blood from the young Apache's face. When he checked the wounds in Chey's body he found a pair of bullet holes. Blood had crusted around the puckered wounds. It told Ballard the Apache had been shot some hours earlier. It also meant the raiders had been gone for a good while.

He walked and studied the mass of tracks that led away from the spread, heading across country.

Who were the raiders? Where were they going?

Most importantly why had they taken Rachel Colter with them?

Less than a half hour later McCall returned with a single mustang on his rope. He dismounted and stood next to Ballard.

'What're you thinking?'

'That Ben is going to come back to this and then head straight out after that bunch.'

McCall tipped his hat back. 'Hell of a homecoming.'

Ballard agreed. He made a decision.

'Jess, I want you to wait for Ben. Tell him what happened. Stay with him whatever he decides.'

'I guess you'll be taking Chey home?'

'He deserves to be with his people. Little enough we can do for him here.

Way he's been hurt I'd be surprised if he lasts more than a couple hours. I'll catch up with you and Ben later.'

*　*　*

After his partner had ridden out with Chey, Jess McCall checked his guns. It was a wise thing to do as far as he was concerned. No time to learn of something wrong just when a man needed his weapons. According to Ballard, Ben Colter would be coming in from the east, so McCall decided to ride in that direction and hope to meet the man sooner rather than later.

He spotted the lone rider a few miles out and eased his horse over to meet him. Colter fit the description Ballard had given his partner. He also recognized the man's wary watch as McCall rode up. The Texan kept his hands in plain sight, away from his sides.

'Chet told me you were not the kind to let a man creep up on you.'

Ben Colter tall, broad across the

shoulders, his fair hair thick and brushing his collar. He had well-defined features, his tanned face curious as he studied McCall through gory-blue eyes. His range clothing was dusty from his ride. Around his lean waist he wore a gunbelt, the holster carrying a wood butted Peacemaker.

'Should I know you?'

'Jess McCall. Me and Chet been partnered for some time now. We were up in this neck of the woods and he said it was time he dropped by to say howdy.'

'Chet Ballard?'

'The same. Colter, things have happened while you been away, and there's no easy way to tell it.'

The lines of Colter's face hardened as he caught sight of the smoke drift over McCall's shoulder.

'That coming from my place?'

McCall nodded. He got no more chance to speak as Colter gigged his horse into motion, pushing it hard as he circled by the Texan and put the horse to a gallop. McCall turned his own horse around and fell in behind Colter.

'That went well,' he said.

Colter was on foot, moving around the area, by the time McCall drew rein and climbed from his own saddle. When he became aware of McCall he turned about and confronted the Texan.

'Where's my wife? Where the hell is she? And Chey?'

'Place was like this when we showed up,' McCall said. 'The Apache was bad hurt. Been shot and clubbed around the head. He managed to tell us a bunch of riders came in. Maybe five, six of them. Wasn't sure. They shot him. Scattered the horses in the corral and put your place to the torch. When they left they took your wife with them . . . '

Colter fixed McCall with a hard look. 'They hurt Rachel?'

'Far as we could figure they just took her away.'

'Chey recognize any of them?'

'He wasn't in a fit state to say a deal. He told us nothing about the riders, or what they wanted. Just that they took your missus.'

'I have to talk to him. Where is Chey?'

'Chet is riding back to Chey's home ground. Said he felt obliged to take him back. Colter — Ben — the Apache was in a bad way. Chet didn't expect him to live out the ride.'

Colter stared around him at the wreckage of his home.

'If I'd been here . . . '

'Not likely you would have been able to do a deal.'

Colter made for his horse. 'Party that big is going to leave a wide trail. I'll find them.' When McCall mounted and fell in alongside, he asked, 'Where you going?'

'With you, son. I got my orders. Chet will catch up later.'

'This isn't your fight.'

'It looks as if it is now. You figure we'd ride off and leave you to deal with it on your own? And not with a lady in trouble. Anyhow with Chet and me along it kind of reduces the odds. Now we going to talk all day or get her done?'

★　★　★

The lookouts had seen him long before he reached the rancheria. News of his imminent arrival was known throughout the encampment even as Chet Ballard rode down through the rocky canyon and across the sun bright slope that overlooked the Apache stronghold.

Drawing rein Ballard took a few moments to study the untidy sprawl of wickiups. Fire pits issued misty spirals of smoke into the pale sky. On the far side of the camp a makeshift corral held a restless bunch of wiry ponies. Ballard's own horse picked up their scent, lifting its head, ears stiffening. Tightening the reins Ballard held the chestnut back. He stroked its neck, speaking to it quietly. Turning in the saddle Ballard took a final look at the blanket wrapped form tied across the back of the pack-mule he was leading. Chey had died a few hours back, never once regaining consciousness.

'*Damn it all to hell,*' he muttered sourly.

Touching his heels against the chestnut's sides he moved on across the slope, angling down to the basin floor. Picking his way through the camp he came under the watchful gaze of the occupants, exchanging greetings with those he knew. Some he now called friends had been enemies in a different time.

Nearing Nante's wickiup Ballard saw the old warrior waiting for him. Nante's seamed brown face was impassive as he stared beyond Ballard to the mustang carrying its motionless burden.

Ballard leaned forward in the saddle, easing his stiff body off the leather.

'It has been a time since you came to visit us, *schichobe*,' Nante said.

'I wish I was bringing better news.'

Nante's bony shoulders sagged briefly. '*Chey?*'

14

Ballard nodded. 'He has the right to be buried by his own people.'

Nante crossed to the horse, laying a weathered hand on the blanket-wrapped form.

'Did he die well?'

'The sign spoke of a fight,' Ballard said. 'Six, maybe more, raiders struck Colter's ranch. They burned the house and scattered all the ponies in the corral. Chey was wounded fighting them. He told me this after I found him. He spoke of how they came and took Colter's wife with them when they left. I was bringing him back but he passed on the ride.'

'The red-haired one?' Nante turned from the horse. '*Aiiee*, Ballard, they will know they have her. I remember the hair and the fire in her eyes.'

Ballard dismounted and stamped around, loosening the knot of muscles in his legs.

'And what of Colter?' Nante asked.

'No sign he's been at the ranch since it happened. My partner is looking for him as we speak. Colter will want to follow the men who did this.'

'Then it is for you to make certain these killers pay for what they have done. *Schichobe*, you have been good to *The People*.'

'And they to me. I have not forgotten what you taught me.'

The Apache way. Blood for blood.

Nante beckoned to some of his people. He spoke and a number of the Apache freed the ropes and removed the body of Chey from the mule's back. Nante watched as Chey was carried away to a place where the women would prepare him for burial.

'Nante, I would have stayed to see him put to rest,' Ballard said, 'but I need to pick up the trail Colter and my partner will leave.'

The Apache nodded. 'You have a good heart, Ballard, and you will be with Chey in spirit.'

Ballard took time to loosen the chestnut's saddle. He led the horse across the dusty basin to the clear, icy stream that meandered from north to south. Letting the chestnut drink Ballard hunkered down on his heels and scooped up cold water to splash over his face. It felt good against his taut, sun browned skin.

Beside him Nante squatted in the dust, tracing lines across the earth with the tips of his stubby fingers.

'These raiders, Ballard? Who are they?'

'Chey said they were *Pinda Lickoyi*. Not Apache,' Ballard said. 'Been thinking about them all the way up here. Can't figure who they might be. Whole thing just doesn't add up.'

Nante listened without interruption.

'I checked the house. They burned it out but didn't loot it. If they were scavengers they missed out on a lot.'

'Then they were fools — or they want Colter to follow them.'

'That was the way I read it. A blind man could pick up their trail. They didn't try to cover it.'

'Then follow them, Ballard, but not

as a blind man. If they are expecting to be trailed make certain to gain the advantage. And ask yourself why they want Colter.'

Straightening up Ballard scrubbed wet hands over his face.

'Damned if I can figure that one either.'

'An old enemy seeking revenge?'

'The ones likely to hold a grudge against him are the kind who use a bullet in the back.'

'*So?*' Nante asked.

'So it's someone who needs something from him. They kill Chey and destroy his house to show they mean business. Taking his wife guarantees Colter will go after them.'

Ballard busied himself with tightening his saddle, inspecting the chestnut before he mounted up.

'Nante, I wanted to tell Tula about Chey. Where is he?'

The old Apache made a sweeping gesture.

'*Quién sabe?* Tula comes and goes

his own way, as always. He is out hunting somewhere beyond the rim. He stays away as much as he can now he carries a price on his head.'

Colter picked up the reins and hauled himself into the saddle.

'Go, Ballard,' Nante said. 'Find these murderers. Bring back Colter and his woman. I will tell Tula.'

'I'll leave the spare horse, Nante. I need to move fast.'

'If I was a younger man I would ride with you, Ballard.'

'They won't go unpunished,' Ballard promised.

'That I never doubted,' the Apache said.

Nante watched Ballard ride out of the camp and vanish in the shadowed cleft of the canyon. Only a thin mist of dust hanging in the air marked his passing. Nante turned as a soft, keening sound broke the stillness of the camp. It was the mother of Chey, mourning the death of her son. Nante sighed. In peace as in war the constant elements still existed. Birth and death. Never far away, and the only equalizing factor between two races. White or brown — all were born and all died under the same sky.

The old Apache envied Ballard his journey. The *Pinda Lickoyi* at least had purpose in his life. Something to add to the dawning of each day. There had been a time when Nante's own existence was spiced with such danger. Those were the times when a man felt the rush of blood through his veins. Felt the hurried beat of his heart. Raising his eyes to the clear sky above the crags of the high mountains Nante allowed his thoughts to drift back through the years. To the time when he had been a young warrior himself. A time before the *Pinda Lickoyi* had shown their faces. Then the Apache had been master in his own land. From the high slopes of the Mogollon Rim to the parched deserts of the southwest. When he had been young, with the others of his tribe, Nante had wandered the Gila

River's course, breathing in the sweet air sent by *Ussen*, the God of the Apache. He had watched the sunrise send its golden light across the lofty peaks and down into the canyons and gorges, streaking the earth with brilliance. At day's end his eyes had seen the wonder of *Ussen's* sunsets dappling the land with many hues of color. He had ridden the Apache trails, shaded from the hot sun by the gently waving branches of the tall sycamores and cottonwoods, and he had known that when death took him *Ussen* would guide him to a place just like this one.

But when the *Pinda Lickoyi* came everything had changed. They wanted to take it all, leaving the Apache nothing. Not content to share the land and its riches, the *Pinda Lickoyi* built their towns and laid railroads. They constructed forts and filled them with soldiers. And then came the betrayal and the lies. The Apache became renegades in their own land. Hunted and slaughtered until sickened by the deceit they fought back. A running battle with the *Pinda Lickoyi*. The invaders had the advantage of numbers and weapons, but the Apache had the land and their intimate knowledge of a hundred secret trails crisscrossing the territory and reaching as far as the Sierra Madre in Mexico. Over the short span of years that the Apache Wars were fought, the inferior numbers of native Americans inflicted telling damage. But the inevitable happened. Outnumbered, plagued by sickness and the constant need to move about, the Apache nation was brought to the surrender table — but never to its knees.

And now, scattered and disbanded, herded about like so many head of cattle, the Apache faced an uncertain future with stoic resignation. Some, like Geronimo, betrayed by the promises of the Army, refused to surrender and fought on. Nante, likewise, took his small band back into the desolate vastness of the Gilas. Here they isolated themselves, counting the days of their freedom which they knew was coming to an end. Some of the younger Apache, realizing that the old days were gone forever and discounting the falsity of waging a useless war, tried to assimilate with the *Pinda Lickoyi*. They took menial jobs, hoping to gain at least a life of bearable peace. Others became scouts for the Army.

The young warrior named Chey, nephew to Tula, had chosen to work with Ben Colter. He had a love of horses and Colter had welcomed his skills.

Colter was a man well known to the Apache of the Gila. He had been a scout for the army, and during the hectic years of conflict he had become accepted as a man of true honor and courage. One of the few the Apache trusted. He had never gone back on his word, or allowed any false dealings to go unpunished. His honesty had placed him at odds with his own superiors, eventually forcing him to quit his job as a scout and to set up his own horse ranch near the headwaters of the Gila.

But now Colter had his own war. His life of peace had been shattered. His home destroyed and his woman taken by the invaders who had also killed Chey. Nante breathed in the fresh, clean air of his beloved mountains, turning his face to the warmth of the sun, and wondered how he would tell Tula his nephew was dead.

★   ★   ★

It was the morning of the following day and Colter and McCall were still following a clear trail. It was almost too clear to be true, beckoning him on, taunting him. Through scrub and lava beds, over salt flats, the scattering of hoof prints remained constant, leading Ben Colter almost as surely as if he was on a halter rope.

The fact that his trail was so well defined annoyed Colter as much as it intrigued him. The men he was trailing appeared to have little respect for his skills. It was almost as if they were attempting to mock him as much as lead him on. By leaving such a heavy trail they were treating him like some newcomer. A fool liable to get lost in his own backyard if there weren't signs aplenty to guide him. On the other hand, if they knew who he was when they hit the ranch, taking his wife and killing Chey, then they must have been aware that Ben Colter's backyard was the very country they were dragging him through. He could have followed the thinnest of trails and not broken sweat. His curiosity nagged him constantly. Colter's mind was full of questions. He wanted to know who had set up this elaborate game. And why. Ben Colter was not a rich man. His wealth, if it could be called that, came from the land that surrounded him. It provided him with everything he would ever need. Materialistic gains meant little to him. Until the raiders destroyed them Colter had his spread and his herd. His wife completed the circle.

Not for the first time Colter found he was thinking about her more than he had previously.

Was she unharmed?

Had they done anything to frighten her?

He found himself smiling at that particular thought. He doubted if anything the raiders could do would frighten her.

If nothing else Rachel Colter was a woman to be reckoned with. Born and raised on the frontier she had faced everything from storms to Apache raids. Her spirit was strong and her character as implacable as the land she had fought all her life. On top of that she was the most beautiful woman Ben Colter had ever known and he was the first to admit that she scared him more than he did her.

Despite his confidence in her ability to weather the storm of her situation, Colter knew that what she faced now would test her faith to the limit.

He reined in, snatching off his hat

and slapping dust from his clothing. The action distracted him for a time, driving Rachel from his mind. He took his canteen and uncapped it, spilling a little of the warm water on his hand. He dampened his lips, letting a few drops slide on to his tongue.

McCall had drawn his own horse up some yards away, studying the ground. Now he eased his long frame from the saddle.

'Look here,' he said, crouching down.

Colter climbed from the saddle and hunkered down to study where McCall was indicating. In amongst the mess of hoof and boot prints the Texan was pointing at those left by high heeled boots. The right one had a run-over heel and the owner wore big spurs. The kind that had those big rowels with spikes. They dragged in the dust wherever he walked. There was one man who wore soft-soled footwear. Could have been moccasins. More than likely they would be the high-legged Apache kind. *N'deh b'keh*. He made out other footprints. The bunch had spent some considerable time, pacing back and forth. Discussing something maybe. *But what?* Colter spotted the stub of a ground out cigar. The dark stain where someone else had spat out tobacco juice.

They pushed upright, tracing the prints, then saw that three riders had broken away from the main group. They had cut off to the south. The main group were still moving east, as they had done since leaving Colter's spread.

They mounted up again. Sat their saddles, staring at the two sets of tracks.

Which one did he take?

The main group?

Or the three who had split off?

Either bunch could have Rachel with them.

Colter made his decision quickly. He would go after the trio. The main group, as ever, was still moving west. He could pick up on them easily enough. But first he had to follow the smaller group in case they did have

Rachel with them. He could not take the risk of bypassing them.

'The three riders,' he said.

McCall nodded and they reined about and set their horses to the south, aware that they might easily be on a fool's errand. Colter decided that he could afford to look foolish as long as he assured himself concerning Rachel's whereabouts.

They rode through the rest of the day and into the dusk. Only then did they stop, making camp in the lee of a rock outcropping. The boulders were still warm from the day's sun. Colter made a small fire and brewed coffee. Cooked food. They ate sparingly and turned in. Neither man said a great deal. They were both aware of what they were taking on. McCall seemed comfortable with his situation.

Colter slept lightly, as always, senses in tune with the land around him. It was a habit he had picked up from the Apache. Resting, yet alert for anything that might present a threat.

There was a need to remain alert, constantly aware of the land and the hostile elements that existed within the land itself and upon it. The Apache had learned long ago to come to terms with his environment. To survive and to use the land to his benefit. That was easier than dealing with man. The elements were a constant. Changing, yes, but within a recognizable framework. The human animal, at best, was unpredictable. Totally without remorse or conscience when it suited his means. He was the only animal walking the earth who could smile and kill at the same time. Deceit and treachery were his bedfellows, and it forced the Apache to walk in a wide circle when they dealt with the *Pinda Lickoyi*. They learned the hard way at first. As time went by and the Apache got the measure of their enemy, they dealt from the same hand.

From those beginnings the Apache, already masters of guile, became better than their enemy. They saw the need for resistance, and for means of survival that would keep them steps ahead in the deadly game. To that end they honed their senses to a higher level, enabling them to survive in conditions of extreme danger. Able to fight on the run. Able to persevere against overwhelming odds. They could strike and escape before anyone realized what had happened. Carrying only the bare necessities they would make their escape into the hostile badlands, urging their ponies to run further and faster than those of their pursuers. And if they lost their mounts the Apache would continue on foot, losing themselves in the barren wastelands. If food ran out they fed off the land. They knew where to find water in the most unlikely places. Sleeping light, resting when it became too hot, and fasting when the need arose. They were characteristics that Ben Colter noticed and copied when he became involved with the Apache. He used those ways of surviving himself, and more than once he had walked out of bad situations when others died.

His following of the Apache ways

brought him problems from his own kind. He was called an Indian lover. A sympathizer. That was foolish talk, especially when it was accepted that Colter was one of the Army's best trackers and scouts during the Apache risings. Colter did his job with a thoroughness his critics could not argue against and in time the talk stopped. But Colter still had his problems. He did see the Apache side and though he fought them, and fought them well, he admired their resistance and the honest way they conducted their affairs. If the government officials and the military had been as honest there could have been a swifter, less bitter end to the matter. But it was not to be. The Apache were cheated and denied even their own lands in defeat. They were shipped off to distant parts of the country where they were made to live out their lives in squalor.

There were exceptions. The warriors who refused to surrender. The likes of Geronimo and Nante. They slipped away to the wild and empty mountain lairs where they had once ruled. Now they were fugitives. Still hunted. On short time. Their freedom was soon to be curtailed, but in those precious months, free from the chains awaiting them if they were captured, the defiant Apache became part of the land again. Free spirits roaming the mountain fastness. Able once more to breathe the clean air and hunt at will.

Ben Colter, now free of the Army himself, might have been able to track down those elusive warriors. He stayed out of the grim game. Content to look to his own business.

Until destiny, in the form of a band of raiders, struck his ranch. Burned his house to the ground. Took his woman. And killed the one Apache who had believed Colter's promise of a new life. A free and independent life if he put aside his thoughts of war.

Now Chey was more than likely dead.

Soon Tula would know about the

death of his nephew. And he would come seeking the killers. Tula was a true Apache. He clung to the old ways, refusing to be swayed. His heart ran true to Apache custom, and Chey's death cried out for vengeance.

As sure as day followed night Tula would come seeking the killers. He would not be swayed. Nor pushed aside — and if it meant going through Colter to reach the killers Tula would do it without pausing for breath. There was nothing as unchangeable as an Apache on a blood hunt.

* * *

McCall and Colter moved out at first light. The three riders were heading in a direction that Colter knew would take them to *Rattigan's Halt*.

Rattigan's Halt edged the bank of a sluggish tributary of the Gila River. It was little more than a drab sprawl of adobe and wood buildings that had been constructed more by need than plan. It served as a trading post cum watering hole for the itinerants of the area. A dirty, unlovely clutch of dingy hovels. Corrals and pig-pens backed up the buildings. Scrawny chickens wandered the area, pecking for food and warding off the emaciated dogs that braved the heat to stalk them.

The man for whom the place had been named — Liam Rattigan — was a tall, shambling Irishman who walked the line between the law and outlawry with a fine step. He was all things to all men. Hiding out the wanted, for a price, then turning on the charm and the moist eye of the law — in the shape of the Army — came sniffing round. He lived close to the edge, facing the world with a smile on his lips and a sharp knife tucked down his boot. He provided a refuge for those who needed it, and charged them handsomely for it. A man under Rattigan's roof knew he was safe. Rattigan protected his boarders, and his genial Irish buffoonery could change to terrifying violence if the occasion demanded.

Colter told McCall about the man. He knew Rattigan of old and he tolerated him because Rattigan wielded influence and garnered information from many sources. The man had his uses. Ever conscious of maintaining his position Rattigan had strong backing in the form of a hard-eyed gunman named Turkey to do his dirty work. Colter had clashed with Turkey on more than one occasion during his days scouting for the Army. The last encounter had left Turkey with a broken arm.

They paused to check out *Rattigan's Halt* from atop a low ridge that overlooked the place. The morning sun traced a coppery finger across the cloudless sky, glinting on the slow water of the tributary. In the far distance mountains humped their way across the horizon, hazy and almost lost in the shimmering air.

Cuffing his stained hat back Colter drifted dust through his fingers as he studied the place. There were horses in the corral. Two women at the water's edge washing clothes. Probably a couple of Rattigan's whores. The man provided most things a weary traveler might require. Smoke spiraled listlessly from the stone chimney of the main building. There was no wind to carry it away so it dispersed slowly, staining the sky.

Standing Colter went to where his horse stood just below the ridge. He opened his saddlebag and pulled out an object wrapped in soft cloth. He revealed a compact telescope. Taking it back with him Colter bellied down in the dust and pulled the telescope to its full extent. He put it to his eye and began a slow search of the Halt.

Movement by one of the adobes caught his attention. He picked up on the shape of a tall man clad in faded pants and a red shirt open to the waist. The man was hatless. His hair was dark and tangled, hanging to his heavy shoulders. As Colter focused in on the figure the man slouched his way from the open door of the adobe and wandered across the yard. A bottle dangled loosely from the fingers of his right hand.

Something made Colter look at the man's feet. The faded pants were tucked into the tops of high-heeled boots. What caught Colter's attention were the big Spanish spurs the man wore. Large rowels, tipped with curving spikes, dragged in the dust with each step. As the man moved away from him Colter spotted that the heel of his right boot was run-over.

He shook his head in astonishment. *As easy as that?* Had he found his three men so easily? Colter passed the glass to McCall, the Texan picking on the man with the run over heel and big spurs.

'Looks like we got him,' he said.

The man with the spurs was joined some time later by a large, burly man who wore a big Navy Colt on his left hip. The pair wandered across the yard and back, deep in conversation. There was no sign of the third member of the group.

Colter wondered, in hope, if the missing one was Rachel. Maybe they had her shut up in one of the huts. Held prisoner — for whatever reason they figured they had.

They returned to their horses and mounted up. Colter rode down towards the scatter of buildings, McCall alongside. As they neared the yard that fronted the main building the two men glanced their way. They showed no sign of recognizing Colter. That fact gave Colter a slight advantage. He drew rein at the hitch post and climbed down, wrapping the reins around the weathered pole. Stepping to the far side of his horse Colter slid his Henry rifle from the leather sheath and made his way inside.

'I'll keep an eye on our two friends,' McCall said.

★ ★ ★

Rattigan's hadn't changed in the year or so since Colter had visited the place last. The interior was shadowed and dusty. Goods were stacked in untidy piles. Blankets. A sorry collection of crumpled shirts and pants. A cask of nails. On shelves were lines of tinned goods. Cans of peaches. Meat. Stone jugs holding molasses. Below them on the floor were barrels of crackers. Flour. A half bag of coffee beans. The warm air lay heavy in his nostrils, mingled odors alternating as he made his way to the rough, scarred bar that was the usual focus of activity. A long wooden trestle table and benches took up the area beyond the bar. Colter saw that he was the only one in the place. He leaned the Henry against the edge of the bar and rapped on the top with his knuckles. After a few moments he saw movement in the room behind the bar, and a tall figure shuffled into sight.

Rattigan was as lean as he was tall. He had a hollow-cheeked face surrounded by lank gray hair. There was a puckered scar marking his left cheek, put there years back by an Apache he had tried to cheat in a deal. When he recognized Colter, Rattigan managed a mirthless smile that revealed his misshapen teeth.

'Who the hell let you off the reservation, Colter?'

'Nice to know you've missed me, Liam.' Colter took a slow look around. 'Place hasn't changed much.'

'My customers like it the way it is. You got problems with that you can always leave.'

Colter heard the soft creak of a floorboard behind him. He didn't show it in his expression.

'How's Turkey?' he asked.

'He's fine, Colter,' came the reply from behind him.

Colter turned and stared at the bitter faced man poised on the balls of his feet only yards away. Turkey, Rattigan's hired gun. A rawboned man with sandy hair and a scrawny, wattled neck that had earned him his name. He wore buckskins that had long ago ceased to be anything but offensive. They were stained and blackened with grease and dirt. Rumor had it that Turkey never took them off. The rank odor emanating from them tended to favor that rumor. The only thing he carried that was clean was the gunbelt hitched around his waist, the .45 Colt nestling in the tied-down holster.

'You got a nerve comin' back here,' Turkey said.

'Take it easy, Turkey, I'm not looking for you this time,' Colter said.

'You still found me.'

'Last time we tangled you ended up with a busted arm,' Colter reminded him. 'You want to make it a matching pair?'

'Ease off, Turkey,' Rattigan said. 'What do you want, Colter?'

'Interested in a couple of your boarders. Pair outside in the yard. Should be another rider with them.'

'Colter, I don't ask questions. They pay the going rate I leave them alone.

That's the way it works. Anyways you don't work for the Army any more. Haven't for a few years. That's right? So maybe your clout ain't so heavy these days.'

'Liam, I never used the Army to back me. Not about to do it now. This is personal.'

Colter picked up his rifle.

Rattigan scowled. 'Don't you go causin' any trouble.'

'You don't want trouble?'

'No.'

'Then let me go my way, Liam. That goes for you as well, Turkey. Deal yourself in you get treated as a full partner.'

'Keep it outside, Colter,' Rattigan said.

'The third rider?'

Rattigan sighed, then decided to answer if it meant keeping any problems out in the yard.

'He took off yesterday afternoon. I heard say he was trailing south.'

If Rattigan was telling the truth, and Colter supposed he was, then Rachel wasn't here after all. That meant the pair outside were the only ones he could get answers from.

Colter stepped out of the building. He narrowed his eyes against the bright sun. He crossed the dusty yard, the Henry held muzzle down at his side, and as he closed in on the two men the one wearing the big spurs turned to face him. McCall moved in to cover the pair himself.

'I know you, mister?' the burly man asked Colter.

'Not as well as you're going to.'

'Hell does that mean?' the burly man asked.

'Ben Colter's the name.'

The burly man immediately went for the gun on his hip. It was a foolish move. Because it immediately associated him with the raiders who had hit Colter's ranch, and it also became a direct challenge. He was fast but not so fast to avoid Colter's response. His fingers had barely brushed the wooden butt when Colter's rifle swept up and round, the metal barrel cracking down across the back of his gun hand. The burly man howled as he felt knuckles crack. Blood squirted from the ragged gash left by the rifle. Colter followed up with a short, hard sideswipe with the stock of the Henry. It clouted the burly man across the side of the face, sending him stumbling forward until he collided with the corral where he hung against the rails. Colter switched his rifle to his left hand, leaving his right clear . . .

. . . Spurs had dropped his whiskey bottle and made a grab for his own weapon. The tip of the barrel cleared leather and Spurs was beginning to feel he'd made it. By this time McCall had made his own move and his Winchester swept round and clubbed Spurs under the jaw. The blow snapped Spurs' teeth together with a jar. He fell back, blood dribbling from the corner of his mouth, his head buzzing from the shock of the blow. Before he could recover McCall hit him again, this time driving the rifle into Spurs' exposed stomach. Whiskey sodden air gusted from Spurs' open mouth as he sagged forward. McCall held back, catching a glimpse of Spurs' left hand dropping to the top of his boot. The hand swept forward, now holding a thick-bladed knife. Spurs grunted with the effort as he slashed in at McCall's exposed stomach. McCall hauled back, sucking in his gut as the keen tip of the knife arced round. There was a moment Spurs was off-balance, trying to fight his own body weight and cut back at his target. McCall didn't give him the chance. He slammed down hard with the stock of his rifle, catching Spurs across the back of his neck. Spurs gave an odd grunt and belly flopped. He hit the ground in a loose, heavy sprawl, and didn't move again. McCall snatched Spurs' revolver from his holster and hurled it over the corral fence. He kicked the dropped knife across the yard . . .

'*Son of a bitch*,' the burly man yelled. He was bleeding from the gash down the side of his face and was hanging against the side of the corral. He had snatched a second pistol from where it rested in his belt at his back. He held it in his left hand, snagging back the hammer as he hauled the weapon into view. A crooked grin turned up the corners of his mouth. That grin was still in place when Colter drew and fired his own weapon in a smooth move that caught them all unaware. His shot struck the man in the chest, punching through to exit between his shoulders. He went down with a thump that raised dust.

'He was mean enough not to let it go,' McCall said.

'He should have thought that out,' Colter said.

Squatting beside Spurs' limp form McCall rolled the man over. He knew from the way Spurs flopped that the man was dead. McCall's blow had broken his neck.

Colter saw Liam Rattigan standing at the door to the post. The Irishman looked back and forth between the two dead men.

'Sweet Jesus, Colter, it's like you never been away.'

'All I wanted was to ask a few questions.'

Rattigan sighed. 'Bucko, when you ask questions the fur always flies.'

'This pair were part of a bunch who hit my place. Burned my buildings to the ground and took my wife away with them.'

'Why'd they do that?'

'That was what I was going to ask this pair.'

'Seems your luck ain't changing for the better,' the sneering voice of Turkey said.

He was standing against the wall, watching with a sour expression on his face.

'Now I don't know you, son,' McCall said quietly, 'but I'm taking against you real fast.'

Turkey eyed the big Texan and decided not to push his luck any further.

★ ★ ★

Ballard had followed the tracks and showed up at Rattigan's Halt short of sundown. By this time the bodies had been buried and Liam Rattigan had been expecting the Texan. He showed little surprise at Ballard's appearance when he walked inside.

'Before you ask,' the Irishman said, 'your friends were here earlier. Ben Colter and a big hombre name of McCall.'

'They find who they were looking for?'

'Two of them. They're planted out back. Third feller had already ridden out. Name of Trinity.'

'Used to trade guns and bad whiskey to the Apache.'

Rattigan handed Ballard a mug of coffee.

'Still does far as I know. Business ain't as good as it used to be what with the Apache broke up and scattered. Mind that crazy buck, Yanno, is still raising hell out of the Sangre de Cristos. Make his raids then vanishes again.'

'You hear what happened at Colter's place?'

'I heard. Bad news for Colter.'

Ballard managed a thin smile. 'I'd say bad news for whoever took his wife and razed his spread.'

'What about Nante? I figure he wouldn't be pleased to hear about Chey.'

'One we should worry about is Tula. Wherever he is he'll be ready to take up the hunt.'

'That is already done.'

Ballard turned at the sound of the deep, slow voice.

And came face to face with a stocky, black haired man clad in a dusty shirt and cotton pants, knee-length *N'de b'keh* adorning his legs. A tight headband held the hair back from his brown face. He stared at Colter through dark, bitter eyes.

Colter knew him well.

The Apache was Chey's uncle.

The warrior called Tula.

'Nante told me you had returned Chey to his people, Ballard. It was a good thing.'

'No more than he deserved, Tula.'

Tula made no move to enter the building. He stood with his rifle resting against his left arm, cradle across his broad chest.

'It has been a long time since you rode along the Gila River with me.'

'We had good days then, Tula.'

'They are gone now, Ballard. *The People* have little left. The soldiers from Fort Brice watch us. They break the old trails and try to keep us herded like cattle.'

Ballard didn't miss the words *try to keep us herded*. The beleaguered Apache, small in number, still resisted and kept the Army busy.

Rattigan appeared with a mug of coffee and took it to Tula. The Apache gave a brusque nod of thanks.

'Colter and a friend of mine have followed the trail left by the raiders,' Ballard said.

'I have seen their tracks. And the trail left by the one called Trinity. I think he is going to rendezvous with Yanno. I have heard Yanno has come down from the mountains to trade. It has been long since he did that. Yanno is loco. He talks the younger men into joining him on the killing trail. Those who are foolish enough will end up dead. Too many have already fallen for his words. If we find him I will put an end to his foolishness.'

'And Trinity might be able to tell me where the raiders are going,' Ballard said.

'You thinking of going after him?' Rattigan said.

'McCall and Colter are on the trail of the others. Might be worth hearing what Trinity has to tell us.'

'I don't see him doing that out of the goodness of his heart, Rattigan said.

'Have to appeal to his sense of fair play.'

Rattigan gave a hearty laugh. 'Good luck with that, boyo.'

'Thanks for the coffee, Liam,' Ballard said.

As he turned from the counter he

caught a glimpse of Turkey stepping from the depths of the trading post.

'*Son of a bitch Apache,*' he yelled. 'What's he doing here?'

As he moved between Ballard and the door, Turkey snatched at his holstered pistol, dogging back the hammer. His face was dark with rage.

'That scalp will be worth plenty and by God I mean to have it.'

Ballard moved fast. In close. His left hand reached out and closed over Turkey's wrist, pulling it to one side. The Colt went off, the slug burning across the store to thud into the far wall. Before Turkey registered what was happening Ballard pulled him round, launched his right fist and punched the man full in the face. The blow was delivered with considerable force, flattening Turkey's nose into a crushed mess that poured blood in red streams. Ballard followed through with a second punch that struck Turkey in the mouth, smashing his lips back into his teeth. Two of them snapped off under the impact. The force of the blow sent Turkey across the floor until he lost his balance and crashed down on his back with a solid thump. The Colt dropped from his limp hand and Ballard scooped it up and tossed it to Rattigan.

'Keep hold of that until he stops seeing two of everything.'

'Jesus, that could be a long time. That idiot never learns from his mistakes.'

'Tula, let's go.'

They crossed the yard and collected their horses. The Apache took the lead as they cut away from *Rattigan's Halt* to pick up the tracks left by the man called Trinity.

*   *   *

They rode until dark fell and then some. Only when the weak moonlight made it difficult even for the Apache did they stop and make camp. Tula found them a place where a cold stream flowed and there was some grass in the trees for the horses.

'I think Trinity goes to the place he has used before to meet Yanno,' Tula said.

'You know where it is?'

'*Ha'oh.*'

'How far?'

'If we ride at sunup only a few hours by your time.'

The Apache was never one to waste energy on too much talk. Ballard figured he had all he was going to get. He pulled his blanket across his shoulders and lay down. Across from him Tula sat with his back against a tree and draped his own blanket over his shoulders.

At first light they broke camp. Ballard checked his horse and saddle, then led it to the stream and allowed it to drink. Tula's horse had already been tended to and the silent Apache had walked off a way to scout the area. Ballard splashed water on his face, took himself a drink and replenished his canteen. When he stood, turning at a faint sound Tula was close by. Ballard allowed himself a thin smile.

'Always the quiet one,' he said.

'It is the Apache way. You were a quick learner yourself, Ballard.'

'You find Trinity's tracks?'

'He leaves a trail a blind man could follow. This one is clumsy. In too much of a hurry. He will not be hard to find.'

They moved out, Tula taking the lead with Ballard keeping watch on their back trail. With the way things were going he wasn't about to get careless.

They were broaching the lower slopes of the jagged mountains now, the day growing bright and hot around them as the sun rose. Tula rode with the sureness of a man who knew his land well. This was home ground for the Apache. The place he had grown up in and with the instinct of a true warrior he rode with confidence.

Ballard realized they were climbing gradually, moving across craggy slopes that brought them into a maze of rocky escarpments and ravines. Around midmorning Tula lifted a hand and waved Ballard to the side. In the shelter of a fall of rock the Apache slid from his horse and beckoned to Ballard. They moved in a silent formation, the Apache slipping from cover to cover like a brown shadow, until he motioned for silence and they peered out from their covering rock.

On the slope in front of them was the man called Trinity, a couple of long wooden crates on the ground. The tops were open, exposing the long shapes of rifles. In amongst the crated weapons were smaller boxes of ammunition. Clustered around the contraband were a small number of Apache. Trinity was in conversation with the wide-shouldered, unusually tall Indian Ballard recognized as Yanno. The Apache was powerfully built, his face mobile as he conversed with Trinity. They seemed to be having a heated discussion about something and Trinity, despite his singularly isolated position, was reluctant to back down from whatever was causing the argument.

'Seems a shame to bust in and break

up the party,' Ballard said.

'I think now is a good moment,' Tula said.

As he spoke he raised his rifle and opened fire. His first shots put two of Yanno's men down.

Ballard followed suit. They were committed now, like it or not, and in a situation like this surprise could make a big difference to the outcome. He hit his first target, the 44–40 slug catching the Apache in the chest and dropping him hard. Ballard's second shot kicked up dirt and he steadied himself before he triggered a third. This time he saw his man fall. Clutching at a bloody side.

For a time, in truth short, there was a vicious crossfire as the Apache targeted where the shooting was coming from. Slugs slammed against the covering rocks, howling off with angry sounds. Two more of Yanno's renegades were dropped to the rocky ground as Ballard and Tula paced themselves to make their shots count. There was a great deal of noise and not a little confusion.

Ballard was keeping an eye out for Trinity. Having to go through Yanno's band simply added a further complication to the task and it was made harder as dust began to boil up in clouds. He lost sight of the man until he saw Trinity, on his horse, emerge from the dust. The man was making an attempt to ride clear.

'Not this time,' Ballard said.

'I will deal with Yanno,' Tula called as he broke from cover and angled in the direction of the remaining Apache.

Ballard saw Trinity urging his horse across the slope. He turned and ran to where he had left his own horse, flinging himself into the saddle and yanking the reins to pull his horse in pursuit of the fleeing man.

He thundered after Trinity, the final gunshots fading behind him as he urged his animal forward. Trinity had broken onto a clear stretch of the slope and was pushing his horse hard. The sound of pursuit must have reached him because Trinity turned to look over his shoulder as Ballard closed in. Trinity had lost his rifle and hauled his revolver round and triggered a wild shot that was wide of the mark.

Ahead the slope leveled out. Trinity turned his horse in that direction, cresting the slope and vanishing from sight. Ballard raced up the slope, disregarding caution and went over the top.

Trinity had reined in the moment he dropped from sight and was waiting. As Ballard thundered into view Trinity swung his own mount around, slamming into Ballard's. The impact jarred Ballard's chestnut. It snorted, shuddering and Ballard felt himself being unseated. He had the sense to clear the stirrups as he left the saddle and fell headlong.

Ballard landed hard, losing his grip on the rifle. He felt himself slide across the ground, half-sprawled, dust fogging the air around him. He heard the heavy thunder of hooves and knew Trinity was still close. Pushing to one knee Colter let his body come round, snagging his pistol from its holster as he sensed the close presence of the horse before he saw it.

Trinity, hauling on the reins to bring his own lunging mount about, was up in his stirrups, swinging his revolver across his body, the muzzle seeking its target even as his horse settled.

They fired together, the shots merging, dulled by the noise surrounding them. Trinity's slug clipped Colter's left side drawing blood in a sudden hot flash of pain. Trinity jerked to the side as he caught Colter's slug in his body. Colter let himself fall back, away from the plunging hooves of Trinity's horse and as he landed he rolled, distancing himself, lining himself for a second shot from the Colt. But Trinity was already falling from his saddle, losing control. Ballard's slug had burned deep into his body. He cleared the saddle and hit the ground hard, bouncing on impact. As Ballard rose to his feet he saw Trinity lurch upright, dust swirling around him as his horse pounded away. There was blood spreading across the front of Trinity's shirt and a wild look in his eyes.

'*Damn you son of a bitch*,' he yelled, his revolver coming round to line up on him.

'Hold it,' Ballard yelled, but knew with cold certainty that Trinity was not going to hold back.

The man's weapon was almost on target and Ballard knew there was no time to deliberate. Ballard triggered his own Colt, felt the weapon jerk in his hand. He fired twice, fast, saw dust spume from Trinity's Nankeen shirt as the heavy .45 slugs struck home. Trinity toppled back with a harsh cry, his own weapon slipping from his fingers.

Ballard clamped a hand to his bleeding side, moving to stand over Trinity. He watched him fade away, and saw his chance to get information die with the man. A bitterness rose in him. All the way he had come and it had resulted in nothing. Trinity had fought to the end, leaving Ballard with no option but to defend himself.

Ballard didn't know how long he stood over Trinity. He failed to notice the shooting had ceased until Tula, leading his horse, came into sight. The Apache had a bloody gash down the left side of his face and there was more blood on his shirt — which turned out not to be his own. He looked down at Trinity's body, then at Ballard.

'He would not speak?'

Ballard shook his head. 'Only with his gun. Wrong choice. How is it with you?'

'Yanno will not lead any more foolish young men into wasteful battles. He too ignored my offer of peace.'

★　★　★

'You had any more time to figure what these fellers want?' McCall asked.

'All I been thinking about,' Colter said. 'That it must be something big to do what they did. Chet always told me I think too much when I have something on my mind.'

'You and Chet go back a way? Both had spells working for the army.'

Colter eased back on his reins, reaching down to free his canteen and take a slow drink. All the time he was checking out the area around them, eyes moving back and forth. He put his canteen away, took off his hat and ran his hand through his thick hair.

'Rachel was due to trim it for me. She's right handy with a pair of scissors. And, yeah, I been thinking about when I scouted for the Army out of Brice. Chet was around too. We were chasing Apache all over. Caught some. Killed some. But I can't see Apache doing something like this. Not their way. Not saying they can't be downright sneaky when they want.'

'You were talking about that one feller — Yanno. Way I heard it he was no friend.'

'True enough,' Colter said. 'Yanno was a mean *hombre*. Be the first to admit that. It just doesn't sit right. Yanno would shoot you soon as he set his sights on a man. But what happened at my place was plain mean. Not how Yanno would do it. And those tracks were made by shod horses, Jess. I'd be plain dumb if I thought Apache never rode shod horses. But not all of them.'

'Son, you're cuttin' down the odds then.'

Colter smiled. 'Hell, Jess, maybe some but not by a lot.'

McCall eased his horse alongside. Looked far beyond the direction they were moving. He pointed towards the distant sawtooth of mountains ahead.

'Sandia range,' Colter said. 'Over to the west it's all rock and pretty desolate. East you've got easier slopes. Well timbered.' He leaned forward to ease his spine. 'Got nothing but a feeling, but I'm pretty sure that's where our bunch is headed.'

They had camped out the previous night, picking up the easy trail in the morning and it was close on noon now.

Colter was good company, despite his worry over his wife, yet now McCall could see he was becoming a shade more tense. He understood the man's concern. Bad enough his home had been destroyed. The Apache working for him killed out of hand. Hard enough for any man to take in. But the worst of it was losing his wife to the raiders. Colter's logic told him they were white men and Ben Colter was no fool.

'We got this pinned down to whites,' McCall said, 'who does that lead you to?'

'I'm no saint, Jess. Had my run ins with a few. Some might still be carrying a bellyful of upset with me. I'd expect them to come for me with a gun their hands. Shooting a man in the back would make more sense than this damn cross-country chase.'

'Sooner or later, son, we're going to find out who this feller is. When we do you can ask him direct what the hell game he's playing.'

'If he's hurt Rachel in any way there

66

might not be any time for him to offer his excuses.'

Colter rode on ahead and McCall could see by the set of his shoulders he meant every word. Colter would want his reckoning and Jess McCall couldn't argue that point. When the raiders took Colter's wife they had crossed the line.

★ ★ ★

'Three riders,' Tula said. 'They are following us.'

Ballard nodded without looking back. 'I picked up on 'em a while back. They're trying to keep out of sight but not making a good job of it.'

'*Pinda Lickoyi* is becoming smarter,' Tula said.

'I had a good teacher. Two good teachers. Nante and my good friend Tula.'

'What shall we do with these clumsy riders?'

'Let them follow until we choose our place to fight.'

'Now I hear the words of Nante.'

'Wise words, *schichobe*.'

'Yes, but, let us not allow caution to draw them into becoming too confident. The words of Tula.'

Ballard took Tula's suggestion, seeing the wisdom there. If the pair following them were intent on harm, and Ballard had already accepted it as close to the truth, then making any move needed to be brought into play quickly. He reverted back to Nante's wisdom.

Ballard and Tula were being stalked. No doubt there. There had been no attempt to make friendly contact, and men who trailed close without announcing themselves had to be judged by their actions.

'The hollow ahead,' Ballard said quietly. 'Soon as we hit the downslope, break apart and leave your saddle. By the time those three react we can be in cover.'

Tula made the briefest of responses.

Now he had addressed the fact they could have hostile men behind them

Ballard experienced a moment of unease. Right now a gun could be pointing at his back. A man's finger already on the trigger. He had to fight back the urge to slam in his heels and kick his horse into motion. A reckless move while he was still in the open. It only took a fraction of time to squeeze that trigger. Less than a heartbeat to send a slug in his direction. The thought formed. Ballard resisted. Kept his actions casual, his gaze on the lip of the hollow which seemed all of a sudden to be a sight further away than it had been. He knew it was an illusion but that didn't make it any less acute in his conscious mind.

As they came to the lip of the hollow both men readied themselves, knowing they had to make their move now . . . and as they urged their horses forward the crash of a shot reached them . . .

★   ★   ★

At six-foot four Vic Parmalee was the taller of the pair. His lanky frame carried little spare flesh over his bones, so his clothes hung loosely. Like his partner Hoyt Sykes his personal appearance was of little interest to Parmalee. His shirt and pants had not seen a washtub in a long time. Likewise Parmalee wasn't a bather. His unshaven face, sunken cheeked and leather tanned, bore the look of a man older than he actually was.

Sykes, a shade over five nine, was bulkier than his partner, with wide shoulders and a tendency to stoop forward. His thick hair hung limply from beneath his shapeless hat, leaving half his face in shadow. He favored a rough beard that never seemed to get to be more than an unsightly stubble. Sykes constantly had a mouthful of chewing tobacco he replenished at regular intervals. He was always spitting out streams of juice that dribbled down his chin and fell onto his shirt front. The never ending chewing had stained his large teeth yellow. Parmalee often found himself wondering how his partner managed to eat and drink when the wad of chaw never seemed to leave his mouth.

Parmalee and Sykes's untidiness didn't extend to the weapons they carried. They were always fully armed. Wore holstered .45 caliber Colt Peacemakers and had .44–40 Winchester repeating rifles in their saddle boots. Matching calibers meant they had interchangeable ammunition. They each had sheathed knives on their belt and Parmalee carried a straight edge razor in a sheath hanging from his neck. Sykes also had a 12-gauge, short-barreled side-by-side shotgun in a sheath on his horse's opposite side. He liked the weapon for close work.

They were unrepentant sociopaths, who carried little regard for anyone. As a pair they were ideally suited, living only for their own personal needs and siding with each other on all things. Neither of them had a shred of compassion. That extended to both men and women. In truth Parmalee and Sykes lived solely for what they could take out of life.

The business of hunting men for the bounty could have been created solely for them. It appealed to their twisted logic. It gave them pleasure and they were paid for doing it. It set them apart from the hardest men. Not that it was of concern to the pair. As long as a man had been posted, along with a reward, Parmalee and Sykes did not worry about moral issues. They hunted and they killed without compunction.

And there was a sideline to their business, though not as lucrative as it had once been. It was scalp hunting Apache. With the reduction in numbers the demand for their hair had shrunk. Even the Mexican outlet had been severely truncated. Not completely but the demand had dwindled.

The elusive Tula, still a wanted man who stayed isolated between his lightening raids, had suddenly shown up following the death of his nephew Chey. The killing of the younger man had brought Tula from his hideout in the remote mountains. He had put himself on the vengeance trail, allying himself with the man called Ballard. With the help of Turkey the bounty team had picked up the information and the trail left by the two men when they had ridden out from *Rattigan's Halt* . . .

★　★　★

To his limited way of thinking, Turkey had a legitimate grievance where Ballard was concerned. The Texan had inflicted considerable damage when he had hit Turkey. His nose was completely crushed and his mouth torn badly. He had also lost a couple of teeth, snapped off and leaving jagged edges. On top of the pain Turkey could barely open his mouth. In simple terms Turkey wanted payback. He wanted Chet Ballard to go through what he was suffering. And Turkey still hadn't forgotten the time Ballard had broken his arm.

When Parmalee and Sykes had

showed up at *Rattigan's Halt*, Turkey had seized the opportunity to maybe make his wish come true. He knew the pair as well as any man could and the moment presented itself when they walked in and ordered a bottle of whiskey.

'What the damn happened to you?' Sykes asked when he saw the damage to Turkey's face. 'You have a losing fight with a buffler?'

'Son of a bitch Indian lover,' Turkey mumbled through swollen lips.

'We know this feller?' Parmalee asked, the mention of *Indian* rousing his interest.

'Name of Ballard. Rode in and done this to me.'

Behind the counter Rattigan said, 'Turkey, let it go.'

'Ain't about to let anything go . . . look at my face . . . '

Rattigan reached out to put a hand on Turkey's shoulder.

'No profit in makin' any more than it is. You pushed Ballard too hard.'

'What Indian we talkin' about here?' Parmalee said.

'I can tell you . . . '

'Drop it, Turkey,' Rattigan warned. 'Let it be . . . '

Turkey spun around, his hand falling to his side, grasping his holstered pistol. All of his anger, built up from the hurt he had suffered, exploded in a moment of pure madness. Without further warning he drew, raised the .45 and put a single slug directly between Liam Rattigan's eyes. The close range sent the lead through Rattigan's head and blew out the back of his skull in a burst of red. Rattigan stepped back, mouth falling open as he dropped to the floor.

'There's one way to end an argument,' Sykes murmured.

He glanced across at his partner who shrugged.

Turkey's patience had come to an end. Bad enough what Ballard had done to him. Rattigan's constant bad mouthing him had finally reached its limit and Turkey had simply reacted.

He lowered his smoking gun and put it away.

'We need to go,' he mumbled. 'I can find Ballard's trail for you. Looks like we all got something to settle.'

He stepped behind the bar and handed full bottles of whiskey to Parmalee and Sykes. Then he searched for and found the metal box where Rattigan kept the proceeds of his trading. It was packed with cash. Paper money and coins. Turkey spread it on the bar top and divided it into three equal piles, offering a stack to each of the bounty men.

'Help yourselves, boys. A donation from Mister Rattigan.'

Turkey searched the goods shelves and found a large bandanna he could wrap around his lower face to protect his injuries. He was thinking ahead. The covering would stop dust irritating his sore face. As hurt as he was Turkey was determined to have his settling with Ballard.

Parmalee suddenly slammed a hard

fist down on the counter to attract Turkey's attention.

'*The Apache?* Hell's teeth, Turkey, who is he?'

'Yeah. Name of Tula. Sure you boys know the name. He's been on the wanted list some long time.'

The bounty pair looked at each other, eyes shining with interest. They knew the name.

Tula.

The Apache had eluded capture for a long time. Using his knowledge of the territory to keep himself from being found. No one had ever come close to locating him. When he wished it he simply vanished and left any pursuers at a loss to where he had gone. He only appeared when he needed something. Food. Ammunition. He knew the old Apache trails. The secret places to hide. Most of the time he lived off the land as the Apache had done long before the *Pinda Lickoyi* had come. In those far off days *The People* had owned the land and everything that lived on it.

They had roamed free, taking what they needed and life had been good. But the coming of the whites had changed all that and in the end the Apache had become outcasts in their own territory.

Tula remained true to his heritage. He followed the way of the Apache. Never asked for anything and only took what he needed. Fate had decreed he would cross swords with the *Pinda Lickoyi* and matters came to a head when he clashed with a wealthy rancher. After a confrontation turned bad and the rancher's son was killed Tula became a wanted man. If the truth had ever been told it would have shown that the younger man had died because, trying to impress his father, he had attempted to restrain Tula. In the struggle that followed the young man died when a gun went off. The rancher only saw his dead son and a hostile Apache. Tula was blamed. A reward was issued, doubled by the rancher. The Apache saw no chance he would be listened to, so he ran. Escaped to the hills and the desolate escarpments of the high divide where a fleeing Apache could hide himself and wander the lonely mountains wondering about the injustice of the white man and his intractable need to crush the Apache underfoot.

Over the long months that saw summer turn to winter and back again to summer, Tula's exile stretched before him with the bleakness of an empty dream that had no end. His only contact with his people came when he was able to visit the camp of Nante. It was during his latest visit he learned about the death of Chey and was able to stand over the body where he pledged to avenge the killing . . . thus eventually bringing him into meeting his old friend Ballard at the place they called *Rattigan's Halt* and from that the joining with Ballard as they followed the trail left by the raiders who had struck Colter's spread, kidnapped his wife and murdered Chey . . .

★   ★   ★

'*Tula*,' Sykes said. 'McKindrick has offered one hell of a bonus on top of the official bounty. We bring Tula in we stand to make a pile, Vic.'

Lowell McKindrick was the wealthy rancher who had lost his son in the clash with Tula and had offered a substantial reward for the Apache's death.

'Turkey, you say you can find his trail?' Parmalee said.

The man nodded. Right then he had said too much and his injured mouth was paining him fiercely.

Parmalee jerked a thumb at the shelves behind the counter.

'Take what we need,' he said to Sykes. 'No sense letting all this go to waste.'

★   ★   ★

An hour later the trio rode away from *Rattigan's Halt* and Turkey, hunched uncomfortably in his saddle, cast around until he found what he was looking for. With Parmalee and Sykes close behind Turkey led the way. Somewhere ahead of them the Apache, Tula, rode with Chet Ballard. If Turkey had his way he and his new partners would catch up with them and have their settlings. With Parmalee and Sykes backing him, Turkey figured he would get what he wanted.

He failed to notice the knowing, silent glances that passed between Parmalee and Sykes. If he had Turkey might not have felt so comfortable in their company. He had no idea his life depended on his ability to find Ballard and Tula, or the fact that once he had located them he would have nothing further to offer Parmalee and Sykes. As far as they were concerned Turkey's usefulness would end the moment he fulfilled his promise.

After that all deals would be off. Turkey would find himself no longer required and the only severance pay he might receive would come out of the barrel of a gun — or the gleaming edge of a killing blade . . .

★   ★   ★

'This is starting to look like Christmas,' Parmalee said. 'First we get to help ourselves to Rattigan's store. Now we got a cache of new rifles to take our pick off.'

'Ammunition as well,' his partner said.

They had come on the dead Apache and the weapons Trinity had been about to trade with them. His own body was found a little distance away.

Turkey cast round and found the final set of tracks leading away from the scene.

'Ballard and Tula,' he said. 'They caught up with Trinity and had their set to. Now they're picking up to go on after the ones who raided Colter's place.'

Parmalee and Sykes were only half listening as they picked through the abandoned weapons, choosing a rifle each. They loaded the weapons, then took as much extra ammunition as they could sensibly carry in their saddlebags. Watching them Turkey stepped forward and picked a new gun for himself.

No point passing up the chance of a new rifle.

He pulled out his old rifle and threw it aside, sliding his new one into the saddle boot. Leading his horse he stood over the body of Trinity.

'You know him?' Sykes asked.

'Name of Trinity. He ran with a hard bunch. Did a little trading with Yanno back there.'

'This bunch you mention? They a problem?'

'Only if they decide they don't like you,' Turkey said.

'Who runs 'em?'

'A feller you don't want to get mad at you. Name of Horn — *Nathan Horn.*'

★ ★ ★

'Any sign?' Nathan Horn asked.

The half-breed Kiowa scout, Snakekiller, simply shook his head. He never used words if a physical gesture could provide the answer. The breed's name came from his skill at killing rattlers with his bare hands. A devious character with few saving graces, he answered only to Horn. With his message delivered Snakekiller crossed to where his horse stood waiting. He took the reins and led the gray across to where the other horses were tethered.

Nathan Horn heard the soft laugh close by and glanced across at Rachel Colter.

'Plan not working, *Mister* Horn?'

'Time yet,' he said.

'Keep telling yourself that and even you might start to believe it.'

The sting in her tone was enough to make him stiffen with frustration. He almost went for her, then checked himself because he knew that was exactly what she wanted. His losing control would simply prove her point about his frustration and Horn couldn't allow that to happen in front of his men. He had been picking up the subdued grumbling from them already. He had been hoping Ben Colter would have taken up the challenge and come after his wife sooner. Horn still believed he would but Colter was taking his sweet time.

'You should know Ben,' Rachel said quietly. 'He isn't going to play your game the way you expect. When he does show up it will be when you least expect it.' She paused. 'All the years you've known him and you still can't figure him out.'

She leaned back against the tree she was sitting beneath, her hands bound in front of her. Though her chestnut colored hair was loose and tousled, her face dust-streaked and her clothes disheveled, Rachel Colter was still a beautiful woman. Her poise was little affected by her position and her ability to maintain her composure threw Horn.

'He'll come and try to free you. When he does I'll take him. And he'll do what I want to save you.'

'You think it'll save *you*?'

This time Horn strode across to

confront her. He was tall, with a solid, yet lean, build. Yet even as he towered over her Rachel simply held his gaze. Not a flicker of fear showed in her hazel flecked eyes.

'I have no intention of hurting you, Rachel. You're only here to bring Ben.'

'Am I supposed to be grateful? Of course, why not. You've only burned my house to the ground and murdered Chey. So nothing to get upset about there.'

Her words, delivered in that firm tone he knew so well, made Horn back off mentally and he stared at her in silence.

'Damnit, Nathan, there's no way back from this.'

She raised echoes of the past. The time when she told him she had made her choice and was going to marry Ben Colter. Then she had used the same tone. Deliberate. Final. Telling him there was no way back from the moment. Then his world had turned dark on him because he knew it was over between them. Whatever future he had hoped for was wiped away by those few words. Delivered as she stood facing him, eyes fixed on his face as she had given him the answer he had despaired of ever hearing.

★   ★   ★

'You can't . . . ,' he had heard himself say. 'Not Ben Colter . . . he's . . . not . . .'

'What, Nathan? Not good enough for me, or not the man you are? Is that the best you can do?'

It was the expression in her eyes that hurt most. He had known his reaction had been wrong in the way he had shown his contempt at her choice.

'Come the day I'll show you who's best. And you'll regret what you just said.'

★   ★   ★

'Tell me, Nathan, is this the day you told me about? The one where you prove to me you are the best? If you think this is the way then I feel sorry for you. All you've done is prove to me I made the right choice when I picked Ben.'

He took a step closer, color rising in his cheeks, and for a fleeting moment Rachel wondered if she had taken that one step too many. She saw his big hands form into fists at his sides, knuckle turning white as he clenched them in barely checked rage.

She refused to look away. Daring him to hit her, yet at the same time fearful he might lose control and strike her.

Horn heard boot steps coming up behind him. He turned, clamping down on the rising anger. The lean figure, wide-brimmed hat tipped back from his stubbled face, gave Rachel a wry smile as he approached.

'She still giving you grief?' he asked.

He was an amiable character, Joe Guthrie, a man who had ridden with Horn for a number of years and seemed to have an insight into the relationship between Horn and Rachel. Nothing seemed to upset him and he always managed to offer her a respectful attitude.

'We were having a meaningful discussion about our positions,' Rachel said. 'Nathan can't seem to grasp it does not exist any longer.'

'Don't mind him, ma'am, he can be a tad slow sometimes. Right enough, Nate?'

Horn struggled to maintain his temper. He was aware Rachel had been deliberately trying to antagonize him. And she was succeeding. As he stared at her he could have sworn there was the faintest of smiles on her lips. He turned away to look at Guthrie.

'You wanted me?'

'Just to let you know that fresh brew of coffee you were asking about is ready. Unless you changed your mind.'

Horn took a deep breath, spun on his heels and walked across the campsite in the direction of the cook fire.

Guthrie caught Rachel's eye. 'Ma'am, don't play your games too hard with him. He has a lot riding on this deal and it's got him by the tail.'

'We wouldn't want to upset him, then, would we.'

'Just remind yourself what he done to that Apache. Kind of suggests how serious he is.'

Guthrie walked away, leaving Rachel to consider her position. She accepted it had been a difficult moment. Brought about by her own stubborn nature. It was something she had difficulty controlling at times. In her present situation she saw keeping her thoughts to herself and her lips tightly shut might work in her favor. That, she realized, was going to be difficult. For some people not so hard — but for Rachel Colter it would be a hard task.

* * *

Dust spumed up from under the hoofs of the horses as Ballard and Tula dropped below the rim of the hollow. The shot that had sounded put a slug through the air between them. As they felt the ground slope beneath them they slid from their saddles and scrambled for cover in the thick brush growing in the hollow.

Ballard heard the rattle of loose stones as their two horses carried on moving, more dust misting the air. He caught a quick glimpse of Tula sliding into cover yards away from where he crouched.

The question in his thoughts was asking who the trio of riders was. Part of the bunch that had struck Colter's place? Had the group split again? He pushed the query aside. Right now the *who* didn't matter. What did matter was the fact he and Tula had been shot at. Whoever the three were they didn't appear friendly.

A rifle opened up. Someone crouching on the lip of the slope was firing down into the hollow. Not taking particular aim. Ballard heard the slugs snapping at the thicket, leaves and branches being shredded as they were hit. It seemed to Ballard the shots were coming from a single source. One rifle out of three. Maybe a distraction while the other two were moving in from opposite directions.

★ ★ ★

It had been Parmalee's idea to split apart. While Turkey laid down a barrage of shots, he and Sykes would take opposite positions and make their approach from left and right. It was no great strategy but it might at least give them an advantage.

Parmalee kept in mind that one of the pair they were facing was an Apache. And not any Indian. Tula was known as a skilled fighter. Any Apache warrior was usually worth his salt. Tula had the edge on that. He had been avoiding capture for some long time. Parmalee took note of that. He might not have had a great deal of time for the Apache. To him they were a source of bounty, but he did understand that Tula was no amateur when it came to resistance.

In the end it was the substantial monetary gain to be had if he and Sykes could haul in Tula's corpse that pushed aside any other concerns. Which in Parmalee's eyes meant everything. He accepted the risk.

As he moved effortlessly through the thicket edging the lip of the hollow, Parmalee's eyes and ears were attuned to every flicker of movement and sound. Stalking a man, Apache or not, was something Parmalee had been doing for a long time. The possibility of getting hurt, even killed, did nothing to deter him. A man lived and died. It was a fact no one could escape, or deny. Death was pre-determined. There was little point trying to avoid it. All a man could do was act in a manner that might extend his life. So taking care how he behaved could mean extending, or shortening, his span.

*   *   *

Turkey had stopped firing. His strategy had allowed Parmalee and Sykes to move forward, searching for their upcoming targets. Parmalee had no idea what Turkey was doing now and didn't concern himself. Rattigan's former employee had served his purpose as far as Parmalee was concerned. What happened to him now didn't concern the bounty man. If he survived the encounter with Ballard and Tula, Turkey was as good as finished anyhow. When the chance presented itself Turkey would end up dead. Parmalee and Sykes were partners. They didn't need or want another partner.

Low down in the undergrowth Parmalee listened. Straining to pick up any sound that didn't belong. He stayed where he was, waiting for the briefest indication of someone's presence. Parmalee had learned long ago how to hold himself immobile. Years of tracking men had taught patience. The ability to remain still while he assessed the situation.

Hoyt Sykes was flat out on the ground, sweat glistening on his face as he studied his surroundings. The only thing about him moving was his jaw, ceaselessly working the wad of tobacco in his mouth back and forth. Unlike his partner, Sykes lacked the calm Parmalee was able to employ. He didn't favor skulking around in the shadows. He would have preferred to be out in the open. He had fired the first shot as he and his partners had spotted Ballard and the Apache. In his haste Sykes' shot had gone wide, fired as it was from the back of a moving horse. All it had achieved was to warn the pair their pursuers were close. That warning had pushed Ballard and Tula into taking cover in the thicket that grew along the base of the hollow. And it was because of that Sykes was being forced to crawl around in the dirt, trying to spot the opposition before they located him.

The thing that worried Sykes most

was the presence of the Apache. He admitted they were good at this kind of thing. Their skill lay in the ability they had to stalk a man until they were a few, unseen, feet from him. He knew that and he didn't like it, not one little bit. Sykes knew enough about the Apache to respect them as frightening opponents. Fierce. Unrelenting and utterly ruthless. Sykes didn't consider himself a coward — but he did value his own life — so suddenly finding himself where he was right now was doing very little to allow him to rest easy. That feeling was not going away until they settled with Tula and he lay dead at their feet. Or the reverse happened.

Damnit, Hoyt, why in hell didn't you make a better shot? A 44–40 slug in that Apache's spine would have solved your problem. Easy to say now. But you didn't do that, you dumb pecker-wood. Ain't no use whinin' over it now, so quit that and go find the sonofa-bitch.

Grasping his rifle he shifted position

to ease the stiffness in his body. As he raised his upper body a few inches, the crown of his hat brushed the overhanging brush. It was a slight movement, barely disturbing the tendrils above his head.

The crash of a shot startled Sykes. The slug ripped through the leaves, passing through Sykes' hat, knocking it from his head and tearing a furrow in his scalp. He rolled aside, panic forcing him to move. It had been that close. Too close. Sykes slid into deeper cover, abandoning any pretense. He burrowed face down, reacting to the burn of pain running across his scalp. He felt warm blood running down from the wound, across the side of his head in a steady stream. It coursed down his cheek and dripped from his chin, soaking into his shirt and Sykes realized how near to death he had just come. He lay still, not daring to move, even though he was aware he had dropped his rifle when the shot hit him. He could see it out the corner of his eye. Just out of reach when he extended his arm. Sykes stared at the Winchester and decided he would leave it for the moment. Damned if he was going to risk another shot. He reached to his side and slid out his handgun, keeping it close. The pain increased, a deep ache swelling from the wound. A second shot drove a slug into the ground only inches away. The shooter was targeting him close now and Sykes figured if he kept up he was going to put a slug into him. More shots followed. Sykes wriggled deeper into the surrounding thicket as the slugs kicked up more spouts of dirt. He pushed his pistol out at arm's length and triggered a couple of shots, then realized he was only making things worse for himself. The shooter already had a fix on his position and his shots were getting closer.

This was getting crazy, Sykes decided. He and Parmalee and Turkey were supposed to be tracking Ballard and his Apache partner. Not this way around. It was wrong. The pairing of Sykes and

Parmalee counted for something. There were few to match them when it came to hunting men for bounty. In truth there was only one man who Sykes would allow might be close. The one they called *The Stalker*. Bodie. Now there was a man Sykes could respect. Hard. Uncompromising. Never let a man get away. Had the knack of setting his trail and sticking to it come hell or high water. Son of a bitch couldn't be bettered.

Damned if Sykes was going to let Bodie's reputation put him off his own game.

He swiped his sleeve over the blood trickling down his face. Then he made his try for his wayward rifle, squirming across the ground and reaching out for it. He closed his hand over the Winchester and dragged it close, jamming his handgun back into the holster as he gathered his knees under him and pushed to his feet.

'*Show your damn face . . .* ' he yelled . . .

And at that moment he heard someone scream. A loud, agonized sound that clutched at his very soul . . .

★   ★   ★

. . . Turkey had heard the shots, close by, the echoing rattle filtering through the undergrowth. They came from somewhere ahead of him so he figured it was either Ballard or Tula doing the firing. He was pushing fresh cartridges into his own rifle so his concentration was focused on that. He had emptied his weapon while Parmalee and Sykes had moved to position themselves. After he had loosed off his distraction shots silence had dropped and Turkey wanted to reload his weapon quickly.

With his weapon reloaded Turkey remained still, searching the way ahead, eyes moving back and forth. He saw nothing. Heard only the returned shots. Then a protracted silence.

It was the quiet that disturbed Turkey more than anything. It played with his mind. Made him wonder what was happening. And not knowing was worse than having someone in view with a ready gun. That Turkey could handle.

He heard nothing, close or far. He saw nothing in the spread of under-growth filling the area around him.

And when he did catch a sense of movement it was near. In fact it was a shadow that slid over him and showed on the ground only inches in front of him. By the time Turkey realized its presence it was too late.

The shadow became larger. Looming over him. And only then did he pick up a whisper of sound. The shadow became larger. Rising over him, dark against the ground.

Turkey raised his head, eyes opening wide as he realized his mistake . . .

He felt something strike him between his shoulders. Felt the penetration that came from the blade of a heavy knife blade sinking deeply into his flesh. For a few seconds he felt no pain, but then it flared. It shocked him. The pain so intense that he screamed, the shriek loud, carrying. Turkey felt the knife blade being withdrawn, then stabbed into him again and again, the thick steel blade hacking into his body over and over. A hand clutched at his sleeve, dragging his shuddering body so he lay on his back, staring up into the grim face of . . .

Tula.

The Apache.

For a moment they were eye to eye, the Apache's face taut with the bitter rage driving him forward.

'Now we will see who takes the scalp, *Pinda Lickoyi.*'

Weakening with every second from the savage knife wounds spilling his blood on the ground beneath him, Turkey was helpless to stop Tula as he bent over, the bloody knife carving an incision that cleaved his forehead in a sweeping curve. The cut bled profusely, streaming down Turkey's face, even as Tula caught a handful of Turkey's long hair and wrenched his scalp clear of his skull. It came free with a wet sound.

Tula held the dripping trophy where Turkey could see it.

The final scream that burst from Turkey's lips lasted as long as it took for Tula to deliver the final blow, the blade of his knife stabbing down into Turkey's chest to reach and pierce his heart . . .

★ ★ ★

. . . *'Show your damn face'* . . .

The shrill screams trailed Sykes' challenge as he swung his rifle in an arc, searching for the shooter.

He saw a dark figure outlined against the greenery. Tall, moving forward, the long shape of a rifle snugged against his shoulder. For a scant second Sykes found himself staring fixedly at the black muzzle.

The single shot came without warning. A .44–40 lead slug that impacted against Sykes' forehead and buried itself in his skull, tearing its way into his brain. He dropped without a sound.

Vic Parmalee slid through the brush, pushing aside the curling greenery, a warning voice telling him something had gone wrong. One minute they were closing in on Ballard and the Apache, Tula, and then things got shaky.

His partner firing off rounds in a rush.

The sudden, high-pitched screaming that had warned Parmalee. He leaned into the brush, eyes searching, ears straining to pick up any sound that might guide him.

At the back of his mind he was beginning to figure he and Sykes had made a mistake. There was something off — even though he couldn't put his finger on what it was. Parmalee immediately thought about Turkey. They should have turned down his offer to come along. At the time it seemed an okay deal. Now Parmalee wasn't so sure. Parmalee and Sykes had never partnered before. They were a two man team and the pairing had always suited them. Allowing Turkey to side with them had broken their accord.

Parmalee moved out of the deeper brush and saw Turkey sprawled out. There was a bloody wound in his chest. Worse was the glistening red mess where his scalp had been torn away. The discarded tangle of flesh and hair lay on the ground a few feet away.

The moment he saw the bloody wound Parmalee thought of Tula.

He snapped his rifle up, turning as a moving shape erupted into view.

The Apache was still wielding his blood slick knife as he ran at Parmalee. Still eager to make another kill.

Not his boy, Parmalee decided.

He eased to a slight crouch, shooting from the hip and hit Tula with hard shots to the body. The Apache stumbled as the slugs struck, weaving to one side and launched the knife with a practiced motion. The knife caught Parmalee in the left side, going in deep and he gasped from the impact. His hands continued to work the Winchester, his shots taking Tula in the chest and dropping him to the ground feet away.

'*You son of a bitch,*' Parmalee said.

He felt the bite of the steel in his body as he moved. Looking down he could see where the handle protruded, some blood starting to ooze from around the blade. Someone had once told him the worst thing a man could do was remove a knife from a wound, especially when it was in such a place. Without medical help he would likely just bleed to death if he did. Not that leaving the damn thing where it was would help either.

Between a rock and a hard place, Parmalee figured. *Damned if he did — damned if he didn't.*

Parmalee heard a soft footfall behind him. He knew without even turning it would be Ballard. His luck was getting worse with every passing moment. He swiveled his head and saw the big Texan edging across the slope. He had his Winchester in his left hand. His other hovered over the holstered .45 he carried.

'This can go one of two ways,' Parmalee said. 'Either of them and somebody gets dead.'

He let his rifle drop to the ground. Kept his body turned away from Ballard so the knife in his side was not visible.

He knew he was going to draw.

What else was there for him?

He also knew he was taking the biggest gamble of his life. If he managed to beat Ballard the knife in his side might still kill him. If he didn't beat the Texan it wouldn't matter anyway.

'*Sykes?*' he asked.

'If that was his name, he played out his string,' Ballard said.

He had seen Turkey's bloody corpse. And Tula stretched out.

'Me and you, then,' Parmalee said.

'What was your deal in this?'

'Sykes and me were after the Apache. Hell of a bounty on him.'

'Turkey?'

'Kind of dealt himself in. Tracked you from Rattigan's place.' Parmalee managed a soft laugh. 'He shot Rattigan before we rode out. Figured he'd taken enough from the man and wanted to move on.'

'Looks to me he didn't get very far.'

'Well, hell, mister, you could say that about yourself . . . '

Parmalee's hand, already close to his holstered pistol, made its move. He drew, half turning his body, head coming round so he could fully see Ballard. His draw, as always, was fast and smooth, but when he went to dog the hammer back he heard a shot. Saw the wink of flame from the big Colt in Ballard's hand. Then he felt the slam of the bullet that thudded into his chest and the pain in his side was over-whelmed by the hurt from Ballard's gun. His pistol slipped from his grasp, falling on the ground at his feet. Parmalee followed it down, landing on his side and the tiredness that rolled over him was just too much to fight so Parmalee didn't even try.

'*Schichobe.*'

Ballard crouched beside the Apache. Tula was breathing slow and deep. His body was wet with fresh blood, the wounds raw and ugly.

'*Ussen* did not look upon me with favor today,' he said. 'My medicine was not strong.'

'Rest,' Ballard said. 'Let your . . . '

A strong hand gripped Ballard's arm. 'My rest will soon be long,' Tula said. 'My foolishness denies me avenging Chey. Now only Ballard can do this thing.'

'I promised Nante when I spoke with him. You know my word was always true.'

Tula nodded slowly. Blood was working its way from his lips. His dark eyes never wavered from Ballard's face.

'Then leave now. There is nothing you can do for me and the trail will grow cold.'

'Leave you like this?'

A bloodied smile edged Tula's mouth. 'Now you speak as *Pinda Lickoyi*, not as an Apache. My death will present my flesh and bones back to the earth. It is where we came from. *Schichobe*, have you not learned anything from us?'

Ballard rose to his feet and walked across the slope, searching until he located Tula's pony. He found the Apache's rifle on the ground where Tula had placed it. he took the rifle and returned to where Tula lay. He placed the rifle in Tula's hands and the Apache grasped the weapon tightly.

'My heart is heavy I cannot do more for my brother,' Ballard said.

'Do what we have already spoken of. Find the one who killed Chey. Who has betrayed Colter and his woman. Do these things and my heart will rest in peace, *schichobe.*'

'If I am able I will return here and take you home.'

'Then I can lie here in peace until you do.'

They were the final words from Tula.

The warrior Apache.
A true brother of *The People*.

★ ★ ★

'I'd say we're getting close,' Colter said.

He held up the dried horse droppings for McCall. The Texan had dismounted as well. It was an excuse to ease his stiff body from the long hours in the saddle. He took the horse apple from Colter's hand.

'Yesterday at least,' he said. 'They're still makin' it easy for us.'

Colter had moved to inspect his own horse, checking its legs for any cuts, or grazes that might prove risky. They had been riding through areas dotted with spreads of heavy brush. McCall followed suit and felt satisfied the chestnut was unmarked.

Taking his canteen Colter swallowed a mouthful of the warm water. He tipped some into his hat and let the horse drink.

'We could do to find fresh water,' he said.

'Right there, son.'

Colter splashed water onto his face to remove the trail dust.

'Something still on your mind?' McCall said.

'It showing that bad?'

'Only when you kind of get quiet and do that staring off into the distance. Which you've been doing a lot of the time.'

'Had that time to do some thinking while we've been riding. About this taking of Rachel and what happened at my spread. We already figured it's to do with me following the trail that's been left . . . '

'Left deliberate to lead you on.'

'Jess, I'm not a rich man. Cash wise I make enough for me and Rachel to live comfortable. Hope to build up my business over the next few years but that takes a while. So what is it I have that makes a man do what's been done? Has to be something at the end. And I might be getting there.'

'There *is* something?'

'Hadn't thought about it in years. Near enough just slipped away 'cause I had other things on my mind. Scouting for the Army. Meeting Rachel and getting married. Building the spread. Hell, Jess, life has a habit of making you concentrate on the day to day things that are important . . . ' Ballard began to remove his possibles bag. 'Late enough to make camp,' he said. 'You want to fix a fire. I could go a mug of coffee.'

From their combined supplies they cooked bacon slices and a pan of beans. Biscuits were part fried in the fat from the bacon. They used water from their canteens to fill a coffee pot. Spooning in Arbuckle's Arioso coffee from a half bag Colter had in his sack. When the coffee had just boiled they added some cold water to settle the grounds. It was no gourmet meal but it suited McCall and Colter.

★   ★   ★

McCall sensed his companion had more to say on his thoughts but didn't raise the subject and waited for Colter to speak.

'Has to do with a story about a hoard of Spanish gold and silver my grandpa learned about years back. He heard the tale from an old Mexican he knew. There was a legend about a Jesuit priest. Back in 1622. A Father Ignacio Corozon. He was supposed to have been leading an expedition of Spanish soldiers who were protecting a great treasure taken from the Mexicans. The expedition was supposed to be taking the hoard to a Spanish fort where it would eventually be sent back to Spain. The story has it the party lost its way completely when they were caught in a great sandstorm that lasted for days. According to the legend they crossed the border and ended up somewhere in what would become New Mexico. They lost men and horses. Became so off their path they had no idea where they were. Led by Corozon they wandered into the mountains until even the faithful soldiers despaired of ever finding their way back. Sick. Weak. Their food and water running out they came on a cave where they hid their gold and silver while they searched for a way out of the mountains.

'My grandpa — Josiah Colter — heard this from an old man he had befriended many years previously. He had done what he could to help the sick old man when he came across him in the badlands. Dying, the Mexican handed my grandfather a map he had drawn, showing the location of this treasure hoard. He said he had found the cave himself many years back. Said the bones of the priest, still in his robes lay in the cave, alongside the gold and silver. He found a letter the priest had written, telling of his lack of hope of ever leaving the place.

'Josiah wanted me to have the hoard. Told me he felt bad 'cause he'd not provided anything while I grew. Hell, he'd given me a home. Clothes. Food.

All this after my folks both died when I was a younker. There was no other family for either of us. We looked out for each other. Became friends. We might not have had much money but he gave me a lot. Taught me how to survive. When he gave me the map he told me to memorize it, then burn it. Keep the directions to myself. He left the decision to me, whether to go look or not.

'Josiah died of a sudden after a long winter. Took a fever and it killed him. After I buried him I figured it was time to move on. I drifted for a time. Worked cattle drives. Anything I took a mind to. Now Josiah and me were both friendly with the Apache. Had a good relationship with them after I pulled Nante out of some trouble one time. It was Nante who told me to sign on and scout for the Army. Said he trusted me to do right by *The People*. He knew the time was coming when the Apache would have to do what the *Pinda Lickoyi* told them. He wanted someone who could talk between the Apache and the whites. Help to give the Apache honor when the time came. I did what I could while I took Army pay. But I could see the way things were going and after a few years I didn't renew my contract. I saw the chance to start trading in horses. There were plenty of wild herds around. Good business in catching them. Breaking them in and selling to ranches and the military. Started small, but built my name, that was around the time I met Rachel. Her pa had his own freighting business and Rachel worked with him in the office. Had a smart head on her shoulders as well as being beautiful. I guess I was smitten from the minute I saw her . . . '

Colter took a breath, reaching down to refill his coffee.

'How did she feel?' McCall asked, sure there was more to the story.

'Nobody was more surprised when she made it clear she had the same feelings. That was where the trouble started. Rachel had another suiter.

Nathan Horn. She made it clear she wanted nothing to do with him. Horn was a wild feller. Ran with a pretty rough bunch and was always close to breaking the law when it suited him. Thing was we were friends. He was the same age as me and he was about the only person who ever sided with me. Even then I knew he was trouble. He was always getting into scrapes. Wanted to drag me along but always stayed away. Whatever we had going for us vanished once Rachel came on the scene. It became ugly. The more Nathan pushed himself on her the more Rachel ignored him. It made him mad. So mad he tried to . . . I showed up at the right moment and we went at it. Battered each other pretty hard until I put him down. I didn't see him for a while after that. Last time I spoke to him he was bitter. Said it wasn't over and one day he'd settle with me. Told me I'd regret what happened over Rachel. Before he rode away he said something that had me puzzled at the time. And there was hate in his eyes when he said it. But the truth is I never thought much more about it. Too much going on. Setting up my business. Marrying Rachel. Been years since it ever crossed my mind.'

'Until now?'

Colter nodded.

'Just before he left he told me when he came back he'd take it all. Rachel and the one thing I thought no one else knew about . . . something Josiah had left me . . . '

'That's what you've been thinking about?'

'Kind of deliberating over it,' Colter said. 'He burns down my house. Kills Chey. Scatters my herd and takes my wife. Leaves a trail I was bound to follow. Man wanted to kill me he could have done it from ambush. Why go to all this trouble unless there's something bigger at the end. And it took a while before I realized the direction we've been drawn to.'

'Where the hoard is located?'

'General area. Got me to thinking. Add it all together and someone wants me in a particular place.'

'You thinking it's Nathan Horn?

'It's all starting to make sense. Nathan Horn has enough knowledge from what I told him before we crossed the line over Rachel. I'd made mention of the hoard and where Josiah had told me it was located. I'd done a fool thing. Talking about it when we'd both been pretty drunk. Now he never mentioned it again, so I figured it had gone from his mind. Plain now it hadn't. Nathan's always had the eye for the easy action. Why work for money when there's a fortune just sitting for the taking. That would suit him just fine. Truth is, Jess, I can't see anyone else doing this but Nathan.'

'And he just needs you to point the finger for the final push.'

'Jess, I could still be way off.'

'And you *could* be on track,' McCall said. 'Pull all the pieces together and the reasons and the ending make sense.

If you're right this feller needs you alive to show him where this Spanish hoard is. Ben, he's using Rachel as his ace. He's gambling you'll do whatever he wants as long as she stays unhurt.'

'And that *hombre* knows me too well,' Colter said. 'He'll figure I'll do exactly what he wants to keep her alive.'

★ ★ ★

Rachel had not been idle, working on the rope binding her wrists as she sat her saddle. She maintained the action, ignoring the discomfort it caused. The thin, coarse binding rubbed at her skin. It didn't stop her. She had determined to try to escape, convincing herself that Nathan Horn, as intent as he was to draw Ben to follow him, wasn't going to do anything that might harm her.

Rachel Colter was ready to admit she could be wrong. That if she tried to escape Horn would have her shot. He had a mercurial temperament and could change from being friendly and amenable, to exhibiting unreasoning anger very quickly. If he thought she was becoming more trouble than she was worth he might simply shoot her. Understanding that cautioned her. It made her realize the fragility of her position. Nevertheless she refused to simply sit by and do nothing.

While they rode, in a long, single file, Rachel took note of her surroundings. They had moved into the lower slopes of a low range of rocky hills. In the far distance higher peaks dominated the skyline. She knew the general lay of the land though where they travelled now was fairly new territory. Ben would know it better. He had a greater knowledge of the country, learned during his time as a scout, and his time with Nate's Apache had taught him more about the terrain. He would be able to follow without much difficulty.

Ben Colter was a man who made little outward show of his skills, yet he possessed a natural ability to grasp a given situation and make the best of it.

In the years she had known him Rachel had become impressed by his quiet competency. The way he adjusted to a problem and solved it, always in his own way and contrary to what was usually expected. She admired him for that as much as she loved him, and now she knew he would come through for her. Somewhere along the back trail he would be riding after her and he *would* find her.

She knew, too, that he would be working out why Nathan Horn had started this. His mind would be going over everything as he figured it out. Which he would. He wouldn't let it lie until he had it clear in his mind.

Rachel was harboring a similar thought.

Why had Nathan Horn kidnapped her?

There had to be more than his thwarted desire for her. Too long had passed for it to still be a driving force in his life. What he might have felt for her must have passed. Or had it? Did he still believe he could win her over? She found it hard to accept. Horn had destroyed her home. Killed Chey. Taken her captive. Accompanied by a group of men he seemed to command. Rachel just couldn't imagine all that being because he still wanted her. There had to be a larger issue.

But what?

What was the secret behind all this?

The secret that also involved her husband.

Rachel imagined she knew everything about Ben Colter. They had always been honest with each other. Never kept anything from the other. Was there something Ben had kept from her? Something that tied him to Nathan Horn. For a moment she was filled with dread. Whatever it was had pushed Horn to extremes. How bad could it be?

Bad enough that Ben had kept it from her, she decided.

It had to be something linking them together. She saw it had to be in the past because Ben and Horn had not been in contact for years.

This secret. How had it come about? And why had Ben kept it from her?

Kept it buried inside. Then something registered in her mind. It felt like a physical blow and for a moment Rachel held her breath.

Yes.

It had to be that.

It all fell into place then. She knew what this was all about.

She had the answer.

It had to be the hidden hoard of gold and silver. The Spanish treasure Ben had told her about. The hoard his uncle, Josiah, had learned about and told Ben where it was located.

Nathan wanted the treasure. And she was the lure to bring Ben into Nathan Horn's hands.

And it made her even more determined to break free and get away from Nathan Horn. If she could do that, go back and find Ben, there would be no need for her husband to clash with

Horn. For Rachel it was all that mattered.

If Horn had no leverage over Ben he would have no reason to continue. Even as she had the thought Rachel understood how Nathan Horn's mind worked. He had already gone to a great deal of trouble to get his hands on her. She began to realize Horn would be unlikely to back away now. He had gone too far. His desire to get his hands on the gold and silver hoard would not let him quit. So her breaking away from him was not going to end the problem.

Damn the man.

He was going to be a threat whether Rachel escaped or not. At least if she returned to Ben's side they could face Horn together. That had to be a better alternative.

Hunched over in her saddle she continued the manipulation of her wrist bindings, holding the reins loosely in her left hand. She was guiding her horse with her thighs and as they were all moving at a slow pace because of the rough ground she found no problem keeping the animal in line. The dun was her own horse. It responded to her as it always did. Horse and rider were well used to each other and the spirited animal took her instructions without hesitation. She had sensed a slackness in the rope a little while back, so she kept up her attempt to free herself. When her right hand began to slip free from the coils Rachel ceased her movement.

She cautioned herself from doing anything too quickly, knowing she was going to need to choose her moment. Despite this she carefully checked out the terrain. The slope away to her left would offer her best chance. The surface was a mix of hard pan and loose talus. A few hundred yards at the base of the slope a spread of cottonwoods would offer cover if she could reach it.

If.

The slope would be tricky to maneuver down. Rachel didn't pretend it would be easy. One misstep by her horse and she might find herself going down. She was going to need to keep her nerve and hope the horse could stay on its feet. The prospect of risking the slope did not put her off. Rachel Colter was an accomplished rider. She had been doing it since her childhood. If she wanted to escape she was going to have to take her chance. She took a quick look ahead. In another quarter mile they would reach the next level and she had no idea what they might be presented with. The slope below her offered at least an opportunity.

A slim one, but at least something.

Rachel took the chance.

As she slid her right wrist free from the binding she took hold of the reins with both hands. She hauled the dun's head round, dug in her heels and gave a strong yell that got the horse moving. It plunged off the trail, hit the slope and under Rachel's urging picked up speed. She heard the rattle of loose stones under the hoofs, leaning back in the saddle as she felt the downward angle of the slope pull at her. Dust misted the air in their wake. She heard angry yells behind her. But no gunfire. Horn would be making his men hold back from using their weapons. A small blessing. There would be no sense in having her shot out of the saddle. Until he decided otherwise Horn needed her alive.

Wind slapped at her face, streaming her hair back. Beneath her she could feel the plunging sway of the horse as it lunged forward. She heard it give a nervous sound as its hoofs clattered and slid over the slope's loose surface, but the animal kept its balance.

For a moment she was tempted to look back to see if any of Horn's men were following. She resisted the urge. Just knowing they were somewhere around was enough to keep her riding.

I won't look until I reach level ground.

She kept to that. Only as the dun, almost stumbling, came to the base of the slope did she throw a glance across her shoulder.

Three riders were coming down the slope. At a far slower rate than she had used. She turned away, feeling the pound of hoofs as she drove her horse full tilt in the direction of the timber. She could see thick brush growing in amongst the cottonwoods. It would all help to provide her with some cover.

'Go,' she yelled, urging the dun on. It lunged forward, applying the full power from its strong body. Rachel leaned across its neck, yelling again. 'Go, go, go.'

She saw the treeline coming up, swinging the dun through the standing timber, the high branches shutting out some of the light. In amongst the trees it was all crisscross shadows, cooler air filled with the scents of the forest. Rachel found she had little need to concentrate on guiding her horse. The dun weaved in and out of the timber, taking them deeper into the thickening stands. The underbrush slapped against horse and rider. Neither of them paid any attention. Rachel knew she would have some bruises to her arms and legs but it was a small price to pay when the alternative could have been a rifle slug piercing her flesh.

They splashed through a shallow stream, cut across a patch of heavy ferns. Rachel caught a glimpse of some dark furred animals scurrying out of their path as they rode through. The dun took them down a dip in the forest floor, cleared a long fallen tree trunk covered in moss, and as it slowed its headlong flight she eased around to check the back trail. There was no movement. No sound. Rachel reined the dun to a stop. Twisted around in the saddle to check.

The forest was quiet apart from some distant bird sound. Rachel slid off the horse, stroking its neck where it stood panting from the wild run.

'Easy, boy,' she said. 'Set easy now.'

She felt the burn of the rope marks on her wrists now. They were raw, some parts moist and bloody. There was little she could do about them now. She had nothing with her. No saddlebags. Not even a canteen of water.

Rachel didn't dwell on that for long. At least she was alive and free. Knowing that she kept her head and didn't allow herself to become too complacent. For all she knew Horn's men could still be around. Staying quiet as they searched for her. She thought about the Kiowa breed — Snakekiller. If Horn set him on her trail life could become difficult.

The other, more important point, was her lack of weapons. Given a gun, hand or long, Rachel Colter could defend herself with the best. She was an excellent shot, having had tuition from her father, then Ben. Even Chey had advised from time to time. She accepted her experience had only been shooting at targets. She had never had to face a human opponent. If it came down to it, she found herself wondering, would she be able to fire on another person? Even if it came down to her life against his. It was a question she hoped she would never have to find out.

She had moved again. On foot and

leading the dun to give it the opportunity to recover from their wild ride. She was moving further into the forest, finding it spread endlessly around her. Through the high canopy of branches the sky was open and cloudless.

The dun's head came up as it picked up scent. It nudged her shoulder with its nose.

'You smell something?'

The horse picked up the pace, seeming to know exactly where it was going and she let it have its head. They came across a wide, flowing stream a few minutes later.

'Might not be a steak with all the trimmings,' Rachel said, 'but right now I'm not complaining.'

She let the dun choose its spot, then knelt herself a little way upstream and took a drink. The water was cold but had the sweetest taste Rachel could recall. She splashed her face, then sunk both hands up to her wrists. The water stung the rope marks but she kept her hands submerged for a couple of minutes.

It was only when the dun nickered gently that she stood upright, turning, and found herself face to face with Snakekiller. Her earlier concern had been correct. Horn had sent the breed looking for her. Snakekiller had a thin smirk on his face, his eyes hot as he looked her body up and down.

'Horn want you alive,' he said. 'Did not say no fun before you go back.'

Rachel fought back against the sick feeling threatening to overwhelm her.

'You stay away from me.'

'You look round. No one here to save you. I send others different way. Only Snakekiller to look after you.' The last words amused him and he gave a raspy laugh. 'Good day for you, woman belong Colter. Today you give yourself to Snakekiller . . .'

He came at her swiftly, his clawing hands reaching for her shirt, tearing at the material. Rachel stepped back, the sickness she had felt turning to anger. As he pawed at her flesh, his stale breath in her face, she pounded at him with her clenched fists and though her blows were solid Snakekiller seemed oblivious. He was forcing her backwards, hooking one foot behind her to push her off balance, and she could feel his rising hardness against her thighs. One strong hand searched for her belt, the other moving over her breasts and she heard the low, guttural sounds coming from him.

No, no, no, she repeated to herself, *this was not going to happen.*

His rasping laughter rose again as they tumbled to the ground, his weight spreading to pin her down. She fought back silently, determined not to allow him to hear her despair. Her fists slammed against his squirming back. He shrugged off her protest. Dragged her shirt open . . .

Rachel's right hand, pushing against him, moved across his lean body, brushed against the handle of the knife sheathed on his belt. For a second the realization failed to register, but when it did she curled her fingers over the corded handle and without a moment's hesitation she pulled the knife free from the sheath. Her arm drew back, the sickness rising as she realized what she was about to do, then she plunged the keen blade into his side, feeling resistance before it slid into his flesh. Snakekiller gave a startled cry as the knife cut deep. He arched his body away from her, but not fast enough to prevent Rachel pulling out the blade and repeating the stabbing motion a number of times. She clamped her lips shut in distaste as hot blood began to surge from the wounds, slick on the knife and on the flesh of her hand.

Snakekiller twisted himself off her, tumbling to the ground, both hands clutching at his bleeding side. He rolled away from her but Rachel, in a rage, went after him and she launched herself across him, the knife rising and falling as she hit him with it again. She caught him in the stomach, wrenching the knife free and doing it again. Snakekiller screamed in pain. Rachel had no idea what she had cut but blood was pumping from the wounds, soaking his shirt and drenching his hands as he tried to stop the flow. Wearied by her frenzied attack she made a final strike, the blood streaked blade sinking into the soft flesh under his jaw. It wedged against bone and she was unable to pull it free. Losing all her resistance she slumped to her knees beside Snakekiller and sat there, her blood-soaked hands resting in her lap, head down. At the time she was unaware that her shirt and pants were streaked and slick with Snakekiller's blood. More had splashed across her face.

She stayed where she was for some time and gradually her breathing calmed and she became aware of her surroundings. The quiet of the forest. The soft champing as the dun cropped at the grass that grew along the banks of the stream. The soft sound of a bird on a nearby branch. She felt the cool touch of the breeze on her face, stirring her hair.

Normality.

Until she glanced down at Snake-killer's body. Bloodsoaked. His eyes wide and staring. His mouth hung open, showing his big brown teeth. The handle of the knife buried in his throat offered the proof of what she had done.

Rachel felt the warm rush of tears forming. She forced them back, willing herself not to give in to the surge of self-pity. Right now she needed to be strong. To remember Nathan Horn and the others. Maybe they would still come looking for her. She had to move. To get away from this place. She pushed to her feet, stumbled to the edge of the stream. She rinsed her hands until all the blood had gone, then sluiced her face and neck. There was nothing she could do about the shirt buttons that had been ripped off, or the blood that soaked her clothing. Leaning over she took a long drink from the stream. As she drank it came to her that Snakekiller must have had a canteen with him.

Rachel walked across the clearing

and began a search for his horse. It was tethered a short distance away. There was a large canteen hanging from the saddle. She decided she would take it and refill it at the stream. A well-used Winchester was housed in a saddle sheath. Rachel slid it out. She ejected the shells it held onto the grass, saw there was a full load and then reloaded. Satisfied with the rifle, she checked the worn saddlebags and found a hide pouch holding extra shells for the Winchester. There were creased and grubby-looking clothes in the pouches, which she threw aside as she searched. Tobacco and a squat bottle of raw whiskey. There was little else of interest. The breed had not carried a handgun. Rachel kept the whiskey and the ammunition. She unsaddled the pony, stripped off the bridle and set the animal free before returning to where her own dun stood waiting. She draped the saddlebags across its back. Her shortcoat was still in place, so she took it and pulled it on, buttoning it over her bloodstained shirt. Taking the canteen she poured out the contents before rinsing it in the stream and refilling it. She hung it from her saddle, mounted the dun and held the Winchester across her lap and and rode out, never once looking back at the body of Snakekiller.

★ ★ ★

Jess McCall and Ben Colter kept moving through the night, taking advantage of a bright moon. It had laid a silver cast over the landscape. The temperature had dropped so they pulled on the thick coats they carried behind their saddles and wore gloves to keep their fingers from getting chilled. They rode at a steady pace, not pushing their horses to avoid the possibility of accidents by stepping into a pothole in the uneven ground.

The Texan was aware of Colter's concern over his missing wife, so he went along with the man's relentless drive to close the distance between them and the kidnappers.

They pushed on with only a couple of stops to rest the horses and give them water, tipping it into their hats from the canteens they carried. The break for the horses allowed McCall and Colter to walk around and ease their own kinks away.

'Coffee wouldn't go amiss,' Colter said.

'So, that is a cruel thing to say right now,' McCall said.

Colter took a drink from his canteen. 'I guess you're right, but I've a powerful craving for a hot brew.'

'We still on track?' McCall asked.

Colter pointed towards the dark peaks ahead of them.

'Sandia Mountains,' he said. 'Last couple of hours we've been taking a cutoff that should bring us a lot closer to where Horn has been heading. By first light I figure we should be picking up his trail.'

'How close?'

'Enough so we'll need to take care we don't just ride into them.'

They allowed another half hour before they set off again. McCall could see the overall darkness starting to fade, pale dawn light revealing their surroundings. He allowed Colter to maintain the lead. The man knew his own terrain and McCall trusted him without question.

The Texan had his own concerns rattling around inside his head. He was thinking about his partner. Chet Ballard was more than capable of taking care of himself. It didn't stop McCall from worrying about him. He would not be completely satisfied until he laid eyes on Ballard again.

First light dissolved the shadows. Ahead were the craggy slopes of the Sandias. Their way was taking them in a direct line now, Colter leading with caution. The air still held the night's chill even as the sun rose. Overhead the sky showed a cloudless expanse that held the promise of another hot day.

In a stand of timber Colter drew rein, indicating to McCall he wanted to make a final weapons check. They each made sure both rifles and handguns were fully loaded. McCall had a second Colt Frontier in his saddlebag and he checked that and fully loaded it as well. They were simply making sure all their weapons were fully functional and ready for use if the occasion arose. It would be too late to have a malfunction in the event of a sudden firefight. McCall had seen good men die because they had failed to make certain they were carrying sound weapons.

Colter leaned against his horse, looking out across the ascending slopes of the mountain range. McCall sensed his mood.

'She'll be waiting for you to show,' he said. 'Ben, you ain't about to let her down.'

Colter fiddled with the pigging strings holding his blanket roll in place.

'Damn if I know,' he said. 'Few days back we were fine. Makin' our way and content. Now our place's gone. We lost a good friend and I lost my wife.' He banged his fist against his saddle, making the horse start. 'All it took was that damned Nathan Horn to move back into our lives ... Jess, I never figured myself a vengeful man, but I tell you now, I'm heading there.'

'Way this is playing out,' McCall said, 'if I get to meet this feller I'm ready to put him down myself.'

'Then you'll need to stand in line. I'm claiming first rights.'

'We'll see, son.'

'And there I was believing you Texicans were all peaceful folk.'

'That we are. Until someone pushes us too far. Then we tend to get all righteous and start to push back. It was what that upstart General Santa Ana didn't figure. Granted we didn't altogether win that one at The Alamo, but it started his downfall. Texas sure did give that *hombre* something to chew on.'

Colter managed a smile. 'Jess, I'm damn glad you're on my side.'

After checking the horses and tightening the saddles, they mounted up and moved out.

Somewhere ahead were the men led

by Nathan Horn. The man was intent on getting his hands on Father Corozon's hoard of gold and silver. Ben Colter was of a mind to prevent that from happening if possible. His priority though was getting Rachel back. If it came to a make or break call, with his wife in the middle, Colter would give Horn what he wanted. He loved his wife too much to put her in absolute danger. When he weighed his options he reluctantly accepted he might have to concede to Horn's demands. Rachel meant more to him than a pile of precious metal. Far more.

Horn had already proved what he was capable of and Colter couldn't see the man backing away now.

Alright, Nathan if this is the way you want it, let it happen. Just think on because if anything happens to Rachel there isn't a big enough piece of country for you to hide in.

Colter let his hand drop to brush against the butt of his holstered Colt.

Not big enough by half.

★　★　★

Middle of the morning and the heat was reaching a peak. The sun bleaching down from a cloudless sky. Radiating off rocks and shimmering in the air around them. There was little chance to escape from it. This was New Mexico at its most merciless. No one could avoid it . . .

★　★　★

'That damn breed should be showing his face by now,' Campbell said, twisting in his saddle.

Hamish Campbell, a long-faced Scot, had little humor. He was a short, broad-bodied man in his late thirties. A mass of thick, curling hair fell to the collar of the striped shirt that had hardly been off his back for months. His unshaven, dour face twisted in a scowl.

'What about Thompson and Ransome?' Joe Guthrie asked. 'They're taking their time. How hard is it to find a woman on her own?'

Horn reined in, clasping his hands around the saddle horn as he stretched in the stirrups.

'That's Rachel Colter you're talking about. Smart as a whip that woman. I'd guess she's giving those boys a damn good run.'

'Damn good run, hell. This ain't a game, Nathan. We're all in this for that Spanish gold. How you goin' to make Colter do what you want if we lose our bargaining chip?'

It was unusual for Joe Guthrie to get serious. It made Horn aware of how important this whole scheme was to the men under his command. They were depending on Corozon's hoard to make them wealthy men. Seeing Rachel Colter break away was diminishing the dream. If they struck rich on the hoard the whole bunch would be set for life — although Horn had his reservations on that. Apart from Guthrie, who did have a brain inside his head, the rest of them would most likely waste any money they made on the vices that tended to rule their pedestrian lives. Drink. Women. Gambling. Horn could imagine any number of them ending up broke again in a few months. There were those men in life destined never to amount to much and the majority of his bunch filled that category. Horn didn't concern himself over that. He had taken them on to provide necessary assistence. They knew the territory and they carried ready guns. He had needed help to carry out the first part of his plan — the razing of Colter's spread, scattering his horses and burning his house. The shooting of the Apache, Chey, had been an added enticement for Colter to follow them — as if the taking of his wife wasn't enough.

For Nathan Horn kidnapping Rachel Colter was a bonus.

Damn right he wanted the gold and silver. It had been his dream for a long time.

But he also wanted his revenge on Colter for taking Rachel from him all those years ago. Horn had *not* got over it. She had turned him down because, for whatever reason, she favored Ben Colter and chose to marry him. Horn had been unable to accept that. In his own eyes he *was* the better man. When Rachel had walked away, into Colter's arms, a dark hole opened in Horn's existence. He was unable to look at any other woman without seeing Rachel, and there was always in the depths of his very being, the conviction that he would one day get her back. Horn refused to face the possibility it would never happen. He still wanted her. Not that he didn't go with other women to satisfy his sexual needs. Bought women. Readily available women. In truth none of them meant a damn thing to him, save for the fleeting pleasure they provided. He used them and moved on, because there was always, just out of reach, his ideal.

Rachel Colter.

Horn had made himself a promise. When his scheme came to fruition, and

Colter had brought him to Corozon's hoard, there were two things he was going to do.

One would be to finally kill the man.

The other would be to take Rachel, by force if need be, and he would have what he had always wanted from her. Even that passing thought excited him for a brief moment.

Horn came back to reality. Before any of his plans could work out he needed Rachel under his control again.

'Spread out. We'll cover our back trail. Let's find out what the hell is going on. Just remember we need that woman alive. Guthrie, with me.'

Horses were reined about. The group dispersed and headed out.

★ ★ ★

It was a time of mixed emotions for Chet Ballard. First the death of Chey. Now Tula. Two good men. Their deaths brought about because of the attack on Ben Colter's place and the kidnapping of Ben's wife. If he and McCall hadn't made their visit to Colter's spread they might never have known what had happened. Not that Ballard felt any resentment over becoming involved. Colter was his friend going back a long time. And friendship meant a great deal to him.

Since leaving Tula, for which he still felt bad, Ballard had ridden almost non-stop. He wanted to locate Colter and Jess McCall. He had a feeling they might be in need of an extra gun. Ballard had no idea what he was riding towards. It made no difference. His friends needed him and that was enough.

The death of Tula would have to be faced when this was over. The Apache deserved his traditional funeral, not abandonment in the middle of nowhere. Apache death ceremonies were sacred things, not to be passed over lightly. Ballard would make his best efforts to see that Tula would receive what was rightly his. The way a warrior met his dying meant a great deal to *The People*. Tula needed to be able to meet *Ussen* in the Apache way.

Chet Ballard meant to see it was honored.

★ ★ ★

Carter Ransome stood over Snakekiller's body, disbelief in his eyes. He took in the scene, the blood dried and caked, the breed's wide-eyed stare. Snakekiller's own knife protruding from his throat. Whatever he might have been expecting this wasn't it. Horn wasn't going to be pleased with Snakekiller dead. The man had been his best tracker.

'I found his saddle and trappings back there,' Cy Thompson said, breaking into his partner's thoughts. 'Horse is gone.'

He was leading his own horse, pausing to scratch a lucifer on the butt of his holstered pistol. He lit the thin, black cigar held between his lips. He stared down at the body with an indifferent expression on his lean face.

'She'll have his rifle then,' Ransome observed.

He rubbed at his unshaven jaw, feeling the rasp of dark stubble. Ransome was hard-faced. Medium height and build. He favored fancy clothes. A bright shirt and striped pants. A large neckerchief that hung its folds down his front. His hat was high crowned, the brim kept flat. Right now his attire was dusty and wrinkled from the long hours in the saddle. Around his waist he wore a hand-tooled Mexican gunrig, the holster sporting a .44 Remington New Model Army revolver. The holster was cut to leave the trigger guard exposed, the butt turned slightly outwards. Ransome had the holster tied down.

'I just hope all this is going to be worth it,' he said. 'We find that hoard it *better* be worth it.'

'You getting jittery?' Thompson asked. He grinned, showing crooked teeth. He blew smoke.

'That damn woman running around with Snakekiller's rifle? Yeah, I'm getting' jittery. Look what she did to the breed.'

'She shore made certain he was dead.'

Ransome pointed out, 'With his own damned knife too. How'd she manage to get hold of that.'

'I figure Snakekiller was occupied with other things,' Thompson said, indicating where the front of the dead man's pants gaped open. 'Too busy with his pecker. That breed never could get his mind off women.'

'You find any tracks?'

Thompson offered a vague wave of his hand. 'Yeah. She went back the way we come in. I'd venture she's gone looking for her old man. We follow her an' with luck we might find both of 'em.'

Ransome crossed to where his horse stood and mounted up. He slid his own rifle from the boot and kept it close. He wasn't going to risk letting the Colter woman catch him napping. If she wanted to play a man's game that was fine with Carter Ransome.

★ ★ ★

They rested in the shade of a wide stand of cottonwoods. The horses bent their heads and contentedly cropped the grass that grew in the area.

'Those tracks are still pretty clear,' McCall said. He was studying the well-defined hoofprints. 'Those boys might as well be leaving handwritten signs for us to follow.'

'Horn knows what he's doing,' Colter said. 'Drawing us in.'

'Must want that hoard pretty bad.'

'Nathan always liked the thought of plenty of money. Thing is he never took to having to work for it. Figured if he could get his hands on it easy he'd go for that.'

'You ever think he'd kill to get what he wanted?'

'Let's say I'm not all that surprised the way things have gone.'

McCall cuffed his hat back. Sleeved his forehead. 'Son, I'm sweating fit to bust. It always so hot around here?'

155

Colter smiled. 'Gets this way sometimes. Likely it'll get cooler now we're
starting to climb.' He indicated the
rugged slope ahead. 'That's the way
we're going.'

McCall surveyed the landscape. 'Ben,
you haven't made my day any easier.'
He raised a hand and pointed. 'You see
that?'

Colter joined him, following in the
direction McCall was indicating.

'Horse and rider. Too far to see who
it is . . . '

The tone of Colter's voice suggested
he might have a feeling who the rider
was.

'Let's go find out,' McCall said and
they mounted up and put their horses
towards the rider.

* * *

'I see her,' Ransome said.

Thompson picked up the small figure
of the single rider on the lower slope.
'Yeah, we got her,' he said.

They put their horses to the rocky slope, negotiating the uneven surface with care. There was a degree of loose shale and eroded sections that made fast riding too risky. As eager as they were to catch up with Rachel Colter, neither man was going to risk a fall that might result in broken limbs — or worse.

By this time they were within rifle range of the lone rider. Under other circumstances they could have fired on Rachel Colter and brought her down. That wasn't about to happen. Horn's orders had been specific.

Capture the woman.

Don't hurt her.

That was the problem. Ransome knew she wouldn't give up without a fight. And damned if she wasn't more than capable of doing that. All Ransom had to recall was Snakekiller.

Horse and rider reached close to the base of the slope.

Movement further out. A pair of riders who had cleared a wide stand of cottonwoods and were cutting across to intersect with the Colter woman.

Ransome squinted his eyes against the sun's glare as the two riders came on. He couldn't yet make out who they were but his instinct told him one of them was Ben Colter.

★   ★   ★

'It's Rachel.'

Colter spurred his horse forward, waving to catch his wife's attention. She saw him herself and responded with a wave of her own, pushing her own horse forward as it reached the base of the slope. Distance closed as they rode towards each other.

Catching up Jess McCall watched the pair of riders still partway up the slope. Still coming. He kept his eyes on them as he brought his horse up to Colter and his wife.

'Are you hurt?' Colter asked, seeing the dark blood stains on her clothing where her coat had been part unbuttoned because of the heat.

Rachel shook her head, hair streaming behind her. 'It's not mine.' She looked at McCall. 'Who's this?'

'Jess McCall, ma'am.'

'Don't shoot him,' Colter said. 'This is Chet's partner. He's been with me since I found out what had happened.'

'Ben, it's Nathan Horn behind everything . . . '

'I figured it out. Why he took you. What he wants.'

'Where's Chet?'

'Somewhere behind us I'm guessing,' McCall said. 'He took the Apache, Chey, back to his people.'

Colter was watching the pair of riders moving in their direction. Rachel turned in her saddle.

'Two of Horn's men,' Rachel said. 'They'll want to take me back.'

'That's not going to happen,' Colter said.

'I don't want to be the one to spoil things,' McCall said, 'but we might have a problem there.'

Colter and Rachel followed his gaze.

More mounted men were converging on their position. Coming from left and right. All armed.

Nathan Horn brought up the rear as the riders converged on them.

'No easy way out of this,' McCall said softly. 'They got us boxed, people, so let's do the right thing and walk soft for now.'

★   ★   ★

By the time Horn edged his horse through his group of riders, McCall, Ballard and Rachel had all been disarmed. He sat facing them, an expression of satisfaction on his face.

'This has turned out to be a good day after all,' he said. 'All my friends gathered in one place. Just like I planned.'

'I like people to be happy,' McCall said.

'Now I know Ben. I know Rachel,' Horn said. 'I have no idea who you are.'

'Jess McCall. From what I've learned you'll be the feller we can blame for all this upset.'

Joe Guthrie said, 'Why don't we just up and shoot this loudmouth? Don't see what we need him for.'

'It's a thought,' Horn agreed.

'Why not, Nathan,' Rachel said. 'Just make it one more reason why I know I was right to turn you down.'

Color flared in Horn's face. He held himself rigid in his saddle as he turned his attention to her.

'That's quite a speech coming from the woman who recently murdered one of my associates.'

'If you mean Snakekiller he got just what he deserved. Given the chance I'd do it again.'

'Just don't let her get her hands on a knife,' Ransome said. 'That little lady is pure hellcat.'

'It appears, Rachel, I underestimated you,' Horn said. 'That can be dealt with later. Let's concentrate on the matter at hand.' He swung round to Colter. 'The little matter of Father Corozon's gold and silver . . . '

'No *nice to see you, Ben?* Where are

your manners, Nathan?'

' . . . that you are going to take us to without any more nonsense,' Horn said without a break.'

'You'll end up shooting us all anyhow,' Rachel said calmly, 'so I don't see why we should make you rich as well.'

Horn took off his hat and ran a hand through his sweat-damp hair. His face went taut with barely-concealed frustration.

'Somebody tie her up again and put a gag over her damn mouth. She is starting to annoy me.'

'Why, Nathan, I recall the time when you only wanted to hold me and . . . '

Rachel's words were cut off when Horn swung his left hand round in a powerful arc. It cracked against the side of her face, the sound loud in the quietness of the empty country. The blow knocked Rachel out of the saddle, dazed, and she hit the ground hard.

'In future, my dear young lady, I'll let you know when I want you to speak.

Ben has allowed you too much freedom. It's time a real man stepped up to teach you how to behave.'

Out the corner of his eye McCall saw Colter tense, ready to react.

'Not the time, son,' he said quietly. 'Don't throw it all away.'

'Take your friend's advice, Ben,' Horn said. 'Just remember who holds the cards in this game.'

Ransome stepped down and dragged Rachel to her feet. Someone passed him a length of rope and he secured her wrists. A neckerchief was tied over her mouth, forcing her lips open as the knot was tightly tied. Ransome boosted her back on her horse.

'It seems your friend, McCall, might be useful after all, Ben. I'd let him advise you to stay calm if I were you.' Horn stared at the Texan. 'Keep him in line, McCall. If he does something stupid I might be forced to shoot you as a warning. Now start proving to me you know where that damned hoard is. I've had enough of this playing around. Joe, you ride up front with Ben and McCall. Anything don't seem right you can take it out on McCall.'

Horn took the reins of Rachel's horse as they moved off. She ignored him, but managed to catch Colter's eye as he rode by. The side of her face where Horn had struck her was starting to show an inflamed bruise and blood ran from the corner of her mouth. Her eyes met his for a moment and she nodded gently.

I'm fine, she was telling him. *Just do what he wants for now.*

McCall caught the look and he felt his admiration for the young woman grow. Subdued as she was Rachel wasn't giving up. The big Texan was thinking along the same lines. As long as they stayed alive there was always a chance. Given that chance McCall would create his own rebellion and Nathan Horn and his bunch were going to feel it when he descended on them.

★ ★ ★

164

Concealed in the stand of cottonwoods Chet Ballard witnessed the tail end of the capture of his friends. He saw the slap that threw Rachel from her saddle and at that moment his big hands gripping the rifle he was holding knuckle-cracked with tension. He had arrived too late to join his partner and Colter and was forced to stay hidden and witness the standoff. It was too far for him to hear anything being said but he could understand from what was happening that there was a situation taking place. When Colter and McCall were placed at the head of the group, leading off, it was plain to see Colter was being made to lead the group.

Where were they going?

And what would he find at the end of their trek. There was still a great deal Chet Ballard didn't understand. He was going to find out. Since he and McCall had ridden in to find Colter's spread razed to the ground and Chey badly wounded there had been a mystery in evidence.

Whatever it was had placed his friends in harm's way. Ballard had to get them away from their captors in order to save their lives and find out what the hell was going on.

He sat his horse and watched the riders take the slope, finally reach the top and vanish from sight. It was only then he moved himself, coaxing the chestnut out of the trees. He kept his rifle handy. If and when the time came there would be no hesitation when it came to using it.

He had his friends to rescue.

And he had Chey and Tula to make a settling for.

Ballard had spent enough time with the Apache to fix his mind on what needed doing for them. What had happened at Colter's ranch had set this whole thing in motion and the men who had led that raid, drawing Tula from his safe haven to make his own vengeful ride, were just as guilty for his death as were the pair of bounty hunters and Turkey. Like the ripples created in a stream by a tossed stone, the expanding circles drew in all who were part of it. Ballard's obligation was pushing him on, taking him towards the time when he would face the men responsible. He did not anticipate enjoying what lay ahead, but he would do whatever became necessary to complete the circle.

Ballard reached the spot where the riders had moved out of sight. He was able to pull his horse behind a fall of splintered rock and see the wide plateau they had reached. He had taken his time, slow-climbing the slope and now he let the chestnut rest. He eased from the saddle, took his canteen and tipped water into his hat for the horse to drink before he slaked his own thirst. He could feel the heat on his back. Heat waves distorted the air.

Even so he was still able to see the group way ahead of him now. They were moving slowly and from the route they were taking Ballard could figure they were aiming for a jagged rise of granite and sandstone. It had to be where they were going. There was nothing else that could have attracted them. Something, somewhere, in the high rocks was their destination.

Ballard watched them. He had jammed his hat back on his head, gaining a little cool comfort from the damp cling.

'*Where the hell are they headed?*'

The chestnut made a gentle sound, alerted by the sound of his voice.

'Horse, it's got me puzzled right enough.'

From the depths of Ballard's subconscious he recalled something that went way back. At the time it had been little more than a few words during a conversation he had had with Colter across a camp fire when they were out scouting for the army. Nothing more than a reference Colter had made when the need for them to ride into the Sandia Mountains had come up. It had only been a passing mention that concerned Colter's grandfather and some vaguery about a long-lost Spanish hoard of gold and silver. It wasn't the first time one of those old legends had cropped up. The southwest had its share of missing treasure. Wealth that had been lost in the empty canyons and rocky escarpments. Hardly any of them ever came to anything. By morning the talk had been forgotten, dismissed as little more than a fanciful tale. Colter himself had never mentioned it again and neither had Ballard.

So was there more to that forgotten talk?

Had Colter's grandfather passed along information to some supposed hoard? Information that someone had taken as true and was now forcing Colter to lead them to it?

'End of the day, horse, there has to be a reason why all this is happening.'

The chestnut chose to ignore Ballard's question and he began to wonder himself if maybe it was the heat getting to him.

He kept his watch on the distant

group. Saw them turn in and start the long, torturous climb up the first of the rocky slopes that would take them ever higher. Ballard realized he wasn't going to need to keep such a close eye on them. He could allow a really big lead to develop before he set off. The way they were going would lead them to high slopes, with nowhere else to go. In truth he could follow them at his leisure. Ballard knew he wouldn't let that happen. His friends were still in a tricky situation. Their captors could turn on them at any given moment. Ballard didn't want to be too far away if things turned nasty.

He gave it another hour before he mounted up and took the chestnut out of cover and picked up the trail. The hard ground didn't offer too much in the way of visible tracks. There were a few faint marks left by the passing horses. Ballard knew where he was going without a heavy trail. His quarry was climbing, moving into the maze of rocks.

Ballard patted the chestnut's neck. 'Let's do this.'

* * *

Behind Ballard, out of his sight, another small group of riders were closing in. They moved with familiar ease, making little impression as they rode. Almost like a passing wind they moved from cover to cover, almost as if they were not really present, bringing themselves closer. They were waiting for their time.

* * *

'No games, Ben,' Horn said. 'Are we near?'

As much as he wanted to stall, Colter knew it wouldn't be his wisest move. He sensed Horn was reaching the end of his patience. If he lost control now the result could be fatal. Rachel and McCall were under the gun right now and Colter knew how close they all were. The men siding Horn were getting as jittery as their leader. If looks could have killed, Colter would have been dead from the scowls they were sending his way.

'He asked you a damn question,' Hamish Campbell snapped. 'You better come up with the right answer.'

'Sooner or later,' Guthrie said, 'you need to make your mind up.'

'If we're close, Ben, tell him,' McCall offered.

Colter sleeved sweat from his face. Raised a hand and swept it across the rock face they were riding level with. He knew exactly where they were. The spot they wanted lay no more than a quarter mile along.

'Close now. You'll have your damned gold and silver soon enough.'

'Now don't you be fooling with me, Ben,' Horn said. 'You point me there right now or I'll put you down, gold or no.'

Colter eased his weary horse forward, allowing it to tread carefully across the loose surface. He knew Horn was riding close behind him, the pistol in his hand pointing at Colter's spine.

Heat burned from the wide sky. Bounced off the high rock face. Even the air they breathed was hot. Colter could feel his shirt clinging to his back, sweat soaking through the material.

He took a look over his shoulder, past Horn to where Rachel and McCall rode in line. Rachel caught his stare and even under the restricting gag he knew she was smiling at him. She sat her saddle upright, defiant, and the sight of her gave him hope.

'Take a long look,' Horn said peevishly. 'Might be your last.'

If Colter could have achieved something, anything, he would have launched himself at the man.

Colter faced front again. As he took his horse over a stony rise in the way he recognized one of the markers his grandfather had mentioned. A splinter of weathered granite with a formation that made it stand out. Despite his situation he felt a rise of anticipation.

He brought the image of the map into his mind. The directions and the location Josiah Colter had detailed. It was all fitting, spreading out in front of him, and Colter knew they were close now. He concentrated on the rising rock face, the granite weathered and shimmering with heat.

Any time now.

He should be able to see the entrance to Father Corozon's cave.

Unless some freak event had occurred. A rock fall. Some natural change that could have blocked the entrance. Here on these high slopes, weather, disturbances, any of them could alter the appearance. Colter scanned the rock face. He knew he was close. The map had indicated so. Colter didn't even consider his grandfather's map to be wrong. Up to this moment everything had been as he described.

Had he, Colter, misread the map?

He was sure he had not. Admittedly it had been a long time ago. Memory could play tricks on a man. Was that what had happened here? A lapse in his recall?

He heard the metallic sound as Horn eared back the hammer of his Colt.

'Time's running out, Ben, same as my patience.'

'Put a slug in his goddam leg,' Ransome said. 'Jesus, Nathan, I'm sorely tired of this *hombre* playin' us for fools.'

'I'll take that under consideration,' Horn said.

Thompson pushed his horse up to where McCall and Rachel sat. He slid his pistol from its holster and levelled it at the Texan.

'The hell with consideration, Horn, time something was done apart from talking. I'm sweating like I'm about to melt here an' tired of listening to you yappin'. Let's see if a slug in this here Texas boy jogs Colter's memory.'

He made to dog back the hammer.

When the shot came it was not from Thompson's gun. The sound reverberated from the rock wall. The slug slammed into the side of Thompson's head, penetrating his skull and pitching him from the saddle. As he fell horses went wild, panicking at the gunshot. Already nervous from the steep climb and uneasy in the simmering heat they jostled and banged into each other, riders cursing as they attempted to pull them back under control.

'Get them calmed down,' Horn yelled.

He had to put away his own gun so he could use both hands on his reins.

Ben Colter took the advantage, hauling in on his own horse's reins and turning it in a tight circle. With uncharacteristic hard action he rammed in his heels and forced the horse forward, bringing it alongside Horn's. Horn reacted, his face taut with anger and he struck out at Colter. He missed his chance as Colter slipped one foot from the stirrup, raised his leg and slammed his boot into Horn's side. Horn gasped as he felt a rib crack under the blow. He slid out of his saddle and pitched to the ground, hitting hard.

Colter left his own saddle, dropping to a crouch over Horn. He snatched the pistol from Horn's holster.

McCall saw his chance. He swiveled in his saddle, kicking his feet free and without a moment's hesitation launched himself at the rider crowding him. The man was Carter Ransome. He had just about brought his own feisty animal back under control when McCall slammed into him. Both men slid over the horse's back and crashed to the hard ground. McCall had landed more or less atop Ransome. With his breath driven from his body Ransome found he was in trouble as the Texan hauled off and rammed a big fist into his face. The blow rocked Ransome's head and he tasted blood from the tear in his mouth. He barely felt the second punch.

McCall pulled the Remington .44 from Ransome's holster, pushing away from the man's limp body. He came upright, conscious of the threatening bodies of milling horses around him.

He heard someone yell. Swung around and saw an armed rider pushing in towards him. The man's pistol fired and McCall felt the slug burn across his left shoulder. It was a passing shot but still had enough impact to push McCall back a step. He pulled on the Remington's hammer and put a shot into the rider. Saw him rear back as the slug hit high on his left side. Before McCall could fire again the rider's head was snapped to one side, bloody debris bursting from his skull as a slug from the unseen shooter struck.

'*Rachel*,' Colter yelled.

'Get her out of here,' McCall called out.

Colter hauled himself back on his horse and as Rachel leaned in towards him he caught hold and pulled her from her saddle, hugging her close. He spurred his horse away from the melee. Hanging onto Rachel as she threatened to slip from his grasp, he let the horse carry them well clear before he reined it to a slithering stop. Allowing her to slide to the ground Colter joined her and turned to face the conflict some distance behind her.

Rachel, despite her bound wrists,

reached up and pulled the neckerchief away, working her stiff jaw. She had no time to catch Colter's attention as he reached out and pushed her to one side, then took the pistol he had taken from Horn and raised it, two handed. When she followed his move she saw Joe Guthrie heading for them, rifle in his hands as he leaned over his horse's neck. His rifle cracked, the slug missing by a wide margin. He was shooting from the back of a moving horse and his aim was off. He raised the rifle again, fired, and this time his shot was closer, spanging off the rock close to Colter's feet. There was almost a smile of triumph on Guthrie's face as he levered and prepared to fire a third time. Colter held his ground, the pistol in his hands steady. He fired twice, very close shots and they both found their target. Guthrie stood up in his stirrups, shock on his face. His rifle flew from his hands. For a moment it seemed he was going to stay on the horse, then he arced back, losing his grip, and went over backwards. He hit the ground with an audible thump. His riderless horse kept going, swerving to one side as it passed Colter and Rachel.

McCall, towering in amongst the milling horses, caught movement and saw Ransome, on his knees, reaching behind for the backup pistol he carried in his belt. It was a short barreled Colt. He brought he revolver round fast in McCall's direction, snagging back the hammer. The Remington in McCall's hand flashed smoke and flame. He fired twice. The .44 slugs hammered home — one in Ransome's throat, the second over his left eye. Ransome fell on his back, kicked in protest before he died.

Of a sudden it became silent. Horses starting to calm down and nothing seemed to happen for a time.

Colter slid his knife from the sheath on his belt and sliced through the bindings on Rachel's wrists. She shook the rope free, flexing her hands.

'Hello, Mister Colter,' she said in a hushed tone.

'Mrs. Colter,' he replied. 'Been a busy few days.

★ ★ ★

McCall pushed by the horses and stared towards the cluster of boulders where the unseen rifleman was concealed. He was not surprised when he saw Chet Ballard step into view, still holding his weapon.

Unshaven, his clothes wrinkled and dust rimed, Ballard was still a welcome sight.

'Son, the next time you have a notion to visit a friend,' McCall said, 'just keep it to yourself.'

'That's all I get for saving your hide?'

'Took your time getting here.'

'Had to find you first. Figured to move in close when I saw what was happening.'

McCall smiled. 'I guess you made up for it with those shots. Hell, son, pretty sharp shooting.'

Ballard indicated the bloody spot on McCall's shoulder. 'I see you managed to get yourself shot again.'

'Only a scratch. Hardly noticed.'

★ ★ ★

In the final confusion Nathan Horn had roused himself, ignoring the blood streaming from the deep gash across his face. He heard the sound of gunfire. The shrill sounds of unnerved horses and the clatter of hoofs on the rocky ground. He understood he had lost control. His men were under fire and he was close to being taken himself. As dazed as he was Horn understood the need to move. To get away from the dusty confusion. He wriggled sideways hoping to avoid any trampling hoofs. His hand brushed something. It was a discarded revolver. Horn grasped it and kept moving. A depression in the rocky surface allowed him some cover and he slid into it, then gathered his legs under him and moved away. It hurt to move, his damaged rib giving him consider-able pain. Horn forced himself to put up with it. Pain meant he was still alive and alive he might yet achieve what he had set out to do.

* * *

'*Where's Horn?*'

Ben Colter stared around as he realized the man was no longer in sight.

'I don't figure he's got far away,' Ballard said.

It was Rachel who picked up on the prone figure crawling along the shallow depression yards away. Something snapped inside as she recognized the man and took long strides until she stood over him.

'Here,' she called out.

Horn pushed himself up on one arm, lifting the pistol he carried.

'Not this time,' Rachel said.

Her right foot kicked out, the toe of her boot catching Horn's gunhand, sending the pistol spinning clear.

'I knew I should have dealt with you . . . ' Horn yelled.

'No chance of that now.'

Horn saw Ben Colter looming over him.

'This is something I've been wanting to do,' Colter said.

He reached own and pulled Horn to his feet, the rage in him giving him strength to stand the man upright.

Colter's hands clenched into fists as he faced the man who had caused him so much grief. In that moment he recalled Chey and Tula. Both dead because of Horn's actions.

And Rachel. Dragged across country like some human bait to draw Colter out. Forced to kill in order to save herself. Bruised and bloodied — but thankfully now safe. Colter couldn't forget, or forgive, that more than anything.

It was all concentrated in the blow he delivered, his heavy fist crashing full into Nathan Horn's face. It split his lips. Blood spurting. Horn's head rocking back under the force of the punch. Colter followed with more, his blows cracking against Horn's jaw, his nose, opening a raw gash over one eye. The beating sent Horn reeling, stumbling back, arms flailing as he made feeble attempts to ward off the relentless attack. He fell, crashing down on the hard ground. Colter bent over him, taking a grip on Horn's shirt that was slick with his own blood. He hauled the man to his feet and dragged him to the mouth of the cave.

'*You still want it?* Corozon's treasure? It's what this is all about . . . so let's go and find what you want.'

Colter had seen the final marker on Josiah's map. Almost a fold in the rock face that concealed the true entrance to the cave. The description was true and it led Colter to the dark opening that had most likely never been seen since Josiah had laid eyes on it in this secluded place. Colter, who had been expecting to find it, was still surprised when he actually laid eyes on it.

Colter literally dragged the stumbling, bloody figure of Nathan Horn and pushed him inside the cave where the Spanish hoard lay in a pile against one wall. Colter thrust the dazed figure in the direction of the hoard.

'Take a look, Nathan. This is it. And you can have it all. Every last piece.'

Horn fell to his knees, sleeving blood from his eyes as he stared at the rotted bags that held the gold and silver. The contents shone dully in the light that spilled inside the cave. To one side lay the yellowed bones and brown robes that were all that remained of Father Ignacio Corozon.

He heard something land close by, turned and saw the pistol he had retrieved earlier.

'Pick it up, Nathan. You want to shoot me? Here's your chance. I'll even turn my back for you. Just remember my friends are outside. You might get me but I wouldn't bank on getting by Ballard or McCall. And Rachel has her hands on a gun as well.' Colter walked to the cave entrance. 'You've got six shots there. When we're gone you've a long way to go and there's no telling who might be waiting to take your gold off you. Six shots . . . think on . . . '

Colter left and a little while later Horn heard the clatter of hoofs as they all rode away. He sat for a long time, his back to the cave wall, letting the pain subside. When he felt able he moved, turning to stare at the piled treasure. It helped his spirits rise as he ran his gaze over the gold and silver.

It was his now. All of it. There was no one else left to share it with.

No one.

He would have laughed but his mouth was too sore. He considered what he was going to have to do. Would Colter have left him a horse? Perhaps he could catch one of the stray animals. Pack the gold on one of them. Enough to set him up so he could outfit himself and come back for the rest.

Thinking about the horses he remembered they would have canteens of water on them. He would need water. Soon. The interior of the cave was hot. Though he wasn't moving he was still sweating. It ran down his face and stung when it touched the torn flesh of his lips.

The thought of water made his thirst worse. That was his priority. Find water. Out the corner of his eye he saw the pistol Colter had thrown him. He eased away from the wall of the cave and crawled on hands and knees until he was able to pick it up. The feel of the heavy weapon in his hand felt good. Reassuring.

Now he needed to stand up and make his way outside. It caused him a great deal of discomfort. His damaged ribs ached with every breath and his face felt badly swollen, slick with drying blood. He had the brassy taste of it in his mouth and he had to fight off the waves of nausea that threatened to make him vomit. He walked to the mouth of the cave, leaning against the warm rock as he stared out at the bright daylight.

He looked around. Saw nothing. Heard nothing.

Yet he had a sudden feeling he was not alone.

The sensation grew as he glanced left

and right. Again he saw no movement. No indication there was anyone in the canyon but himself.

And then the words came. Seemingly out of nowhere.

'*We are here, Pinda Lickoyi, and we have come for you . . .* '

★ ★ ★

They had moved on silent feet, barely a whisper as they converged on the spot. Even in the hard glare of the sun there was no sight of them as they flitted from rock to rock. No speech, yet they each knew what the others wanted as they closed in.

Led by Nante, old as he was, the Apache came to the cave and gathered at the narrow entrance. There were no more than six of them, stocky built, lean and brown, dressed in their cotton shirts and breechclouts, legs covered by knee-length *N'deh b'keh*. Headbands held their shoulder length black hair away from expressionless faces.

Between them they carried an assortment of weapons. Mostly well-used but cared for rifles of differing vintages. Lever action Winchesters. Henrys. Seven shot .56–56 caliber Spencer Repeating rifles. Some were decorated with brass headed nails driven into the wood stocks. Each warrior carried a broad-bladed knife in sheaths. One of them had a bow with a full quiver holding hand-crafted arrows. The quiver was carried across the man's broad back.

'*Pinda Lickoyi*, come and face us,' Nante called. 'We have words for you, murderer of Chey.'

From inside the cave there was a sound of movement.

The crash of a pistol shot came then, the slug passing harmlessly because the Apache were standing to the sides of the entrance.

'*Pinda Lickoyi* there is no escape. Nowhere to run for a coward . . . '

A second shot came.

The sound of someone moving around inside the cave.

'They call you Na-tan. Na-tan Horn. I have spoken with my friend Colter. He has given me the words on your treachery. How you destroyed his home and took his woman. And you killed my nephew, Chey. Because of what you did Tula followed and he is also dead, so there is much on your shoulders, Na-tan Horn. Now your deceit has brought death to the ones who rode with you. Colter and his woman are free and going home. And you, Na-tan Horn, you have your gold. We will go and leave you with it. As you wished you have your treasure. Here you can be with it for the rest of your life . . . '

Twice more the hidden gun fired, the brief muzzle flashes showing in the shadows beyond the opening.

'Go to hell, you sons of bitches. *I ain't coming out.*'

The ghost of a smile flickered across Nante's grim features.

'Of that I am certain, *Pinda Lickoyi.*'

Nante raised a hand to the pair of Apache, climbed up and perched on the rock face over the cave entrance. They moved to use the thick lengths of timber they carried and began to lever at the splintered slabs of granite behind which they stood. At first their efforts were ineffectual, but their persistence paid off. First it was a faint trace of dust and loose stones slipping free and cascading down the rock face. Once they had purchase they were able to dig in beneath larger chunks of rock. Larger pieces broke off. Fractured sections that slid free and tumbled down, trailing more dust. The sweating pair thrust their levers in deeper, finding larger, heavier fractured rock and began to move a wedged mass.

Nante took his warriors back, clear of the entrance to the cave as more and more debris came down. He stood watching in silent approval as the cascade increased. The fallen rocks began to build at the cave entrance. Dust fogged the air.

From inside a wail of despair reached Nante's ears as Horn realized the true intent of what was happening.

'*No . . . you can't . . . I'll give you the gold . . .* '

The plea was cut off in the heavy rumble as the laboring Apache finally loosened the mass of rock. As it slid away from them they quickly scrambled away to avoid being taken by the rock fall they had created.

The resultant avalanche was spectacular. Tons of larger boulders and slabs of granite came crashing down, piling up around the cave entrance, spreading out across the ground in either direction. Smaller rocks bounded free and the rock fall piled up. The fall continued for long minutes, dusting the hot air and when it cleared away the section around the entrance had been altered beyond recognition.

Nante remained watching until the dust cleared, nodding in silent satisfaction. He raised a hand to his waiting warriors.

'The *Pinda Lickoyi* has his treasure. Let us go and find Tula. We will take him home. Where he can be with his family . . . '

★   ★   ★

Dust had billowed back into the cave. It caught Nathan Horn's throat and set him coughing harshly. Any light that might have filtered inside the cave earlier was gone now, blocked off by the massive fall of rock that effectively sealed the cave. The massive rock fall, bringing down those tons of granite would never be moved. He was here to stay. The darkness was absolute. Horn couldn't even see his hand when he held it close to his face. In the panic that had overtaken him as the rock fall took place he had dropped the pistol. He fell to his knees now, searching in the darkness.

He had to find the gun. There was one cartridge left in the cylinder. Even though he felt sick at the thought he knew the gun offered him a way out. Horn knew he would not be able to break free from the cave. The Apache had made sure of that. They might not have pulled a trigger on him but they had condemned him to death as surely as they might have if they had shot him.

He stumbled back and forth, scraping the flesh of his hands on the cave floor as he searched for the elusive pistol. At one point he located the leather satchels holding the Spanish gold and silver. He felt tears scald his cheeks as he touched them. All the wealth around him and it was useless.

Horn turned himself around and began to search again for the pistol. He had to find it. Surely if he kept searching he would locate it.

A harsh chuckle escaped his lips.

He would find it eventually.

He had all the time in the world . . . the finality of his situation came to him and he hung his head and wept . . .

★ ★ ★

Only the brittle scratching of the quill moving across the parchment

broke the silence of the canyon. Tiny dust motes danced within the shimmering waves of heat, dipping and rising on gentle air currents.

High above the solid walls of ochre colored stone hung a strip of blue-washed sky. Empty. Cloudless.

The scratching ceased. The quill paused as the writer's train of thought wandered, returning the canyon to total silence once again.

And then . . .

'God save me from this terrible place!'

BALLARD & McCALL:
TWO FROM TEXAS
GUNS OF THE BRASADA
COLORADO BLOOD HUNT

We do hope that you have enjoyed reading this large print book.

Did you know that all of our titles are available for purchase?

We publish a wide range of high quality large print books including:
Romances, Mysteries, Classics
General Fiction
Non Fiction and Westerns

Special interest titles available in large print are:
The Little Oxford Dictionary
Music Book, Song Book
Hymn Book, Service Book

Also available from us courtesy of Oxford University Press:
Young Readers' Dictionary
(large print edition)
Young Readers' Thesaurus
(large print edition)

For further information or a free brochure, please contact us at:
Ulverscroft Large Print Books Ltd.,
The Green, Bradgate Road, Anstey,
Leicester, LE7 7FU, England.
Tel: (00 44) **0116 236 4325**
Fax: (00 44) **0116 234 0205**

Other titles in the
Linford Western Library:

BLIZZARD JUSTICE

Randolph Vincent

After frostbite crippled the fingers of his gun hand, Isaac Morgan thought his days of chasing desperadoes were over. But when steel-hearted Deputy US Marshal Ambrose Bishop rides into town one winter evening, aiming to bait a trap for a brutal gang which has been terrorizing the border, Morgan's peace is shattered. For after the lawman's scheme misfires, and the miscreants snatch the town judge's beautiful daughter Kitty, Bishop and Morgan must join forces to get her back.

DYNAMITE EXPRESS

Gillian F. Taylor

Sheriff Alec Lawson has come a long way from the Scottish Highlands to Colorado. Life here is never slow as he deals with a kidnapped Chinese woman, moonshine that's turning its consumers blind, and a terrifying incident with an uncoupled locomotive which sees him clinging to the roof of a speeding train car. When a man is found dead out in the wild, Lawson wonders if the witness is telling him the whole truth, and decides to dig a little deeper . . .

HANGING DAY

Rob Hill

Facing the noose after being wrong-fully convicted of his wife's murder, Josh Tillman breaks out of jail. Rather than go on the run, he heads home, determined to prove his innocence and track down the real killer. But he has no evidence or witnesses to back up his story; his father-in-law wants him dead; a corrupt prison guard is pursuing him; and the preacher who speaks out in his defence is held at gunpoint for his trouble . . .